HURTS SO GOOD

Also by Alison Tyler:

A Is for Amour
B Is for Bondage
Best Bondage Erotica
Best Bondage Erotica, Volume 2
C Is for Coeds
Caught Looking (with Rachel Kramer Bussel)
D Is for Dress-Up
E Is for Exotic
Exposed
Frenzy
G Is for Games
Got a Minute?
H Is for Hardcore
Hide and Seek (with Rachel Kramer Bussel)
The Happy Birthday Book of Erotica
Heat Wave
I Is for Indecent
J Is for Jealousy
K Is for Kinky
L Is for Leather
Love at First Sting
Luscious
The Merry XXXmas Book of Erotica
Naughty or Nice
Never Have the Same Sex Twice
Open for Business
Red Hot Erotica
Slave to Love
Three-way

HURTS SO GOOD

UNRESTRAINED EROTICA

Edited by
Alison Tyler

Foreword by
Barbara pizio

CLEiS
PRESS

Published in the United States by Cleis Press Inc.,
2246 Sixth St., Berkeley, CA 94710

Printed in the United States.
Cover design: Scott Ideleman/Blink
Cover photograph: Roman Kasperski
Text design: Frank Wiedemann

Second Edition.
10 9 8 7 6 5 4 3 2 1

Trade paper ISBN: 978-1-57344-723-2
E-book ISBN: 978-1-57344-743-0

Dedicated to Sam

Penthouse Variations™ is a trademark of General Media Communications, Inc. Used by permission.

Contents

FOREWORD

Hurts so good—at face value, it seems to be a contradiction. But the art of power exchange—the heart and soul of BDSM—is its own special type of alchemy, creating a dreamy world where pain equals pleasure and bondage means freedom.

Consider the position a submissive willingly puts himself in: bound and helpless, facing all of his dreams and fears as well as his mistress's lash. Nevermind the leather—clothed or naked, he is stripped down to his most basic physical and emotional needs in his quest to relinquish control and expose himself to an extreme range of feelings and sensations.

As time seems to slow, drawing out the moments between beats of his heart, he confronts his warring desires and his world is reduced to what she allows him to experience: the snug embrace of his restraints, the ticklish tease of her fingernails being drawn across his flesh, the hot rush of her breath against the back of his neck. Anticipation is a heady elixir, whetting his erotic appetite even as nervousness swells inside him.

Without warning, the snap of leather against skin offers a loud report, like a bright flash of lightning before the rumbling thunder strike. A split second later, the impact of that expertly placed lash resonates as a sharp spark within him, the heat building as she takes him higher and higher with each additional stroke.

And as he accepts her gift of pain—testing his will and striving toward the bliss of release—he is the furthest thing from weak.

It takes tremendous strength, resolve and trust to put yourself completely in the hands of another person—one whom you know with absolute certainty is going to push your limits, physically and emotionally. But it's this swirl of sensations and feelings that combine in a perfect storm of kink and makes the seemingly impossible not only occur, but happen in a way that creates a sexy good time for everyone involved. As the editor of *Penthouse Variations*™ magazine, I receive letters every day from readers who not only understand these seemingly conflicting worlds but experience their pleasures first-hand.

The sensual stories that Alison Tyler has assembled in this collection delve into the dynamics of relationships filled with such unrestrained passion, revealing a world of beautiful contradictions that will thrill and inspire you.

Some of these tales show how the everyday can be instantly transformed into pulse-quickening moments laced with eroticism. Sommer Marsden's "Panty Lines" and Jay Lawrence's "Provocation" reflect the experiences of couples that work episodes of power play into their daily lives, momentarily enjoying the thrill of the game and then returning to their usual roles.

Other stories in this anthology, like Morgan Aine's "Party Manners" and Xan West's "First Time Since," reveal the emotions at play beneath more intense D/s relationships. These authors tell tales of deeply passionate experiences, and the payoff for these characters is directly commensurate with the depth of their emotional investment. These darker fantasies complement the light, allowing this collection to reveal a full spectrum of experiences within the world of S/M.

Read through these sinfully decadent tales and let their words wash over you. Each story will build upon the next, their erotic episodes fleshing out a complex portrait of passion as they embrace the pleasurable paradox of kink and its many luscious possibilities.

Barbara Pizio
Executive Editor
Penthouse Variations™

INTRODUCTION:
NO APOLOGIES

Kink makes me come. Always has. I've learned to embrace the fact that I like to play with pain + pleasure. More than simply wrapping my mind around the concept of BDSM behavior, I've wrapped my legs, my arms, my whole body. But kink does more than take me to my outer limits. Kink calms me down.

Generally, I juggle like a pro. I've been known to keep six projects in the air simultaneously, without missing a beat. Without dropping the brightly colored balls. *Look at me,* I want to shout. *Look at this!*

But then there are days when I run around feeling frantic, alighting on one activity after another without giving my full focus to any one. Without being able to finish a fucking thing. It's times like these, when my thoughts spiral through my mind at top speed, that I most crave the spark, the spike, that hot-wax feeling of pain mixed with pleasure. Because even if I never shut down my mind altogether, even if I never grow fully quiet during an erotic scene, kink does something for me.

It anchors me.

I can't think about those six projects if I'm tied to a bed, wondering when the whip will fall. I can't throw the balls into the air if my hands are cuffed and a velvety blindfold is draped over my eyes.

The constant noise in my head is silenced, so that I pay attention. So that something else takes precedence. Diana St. John knows exactly what I mean. She says in her delicious story "Omega to Alpha": *What was more memorable was the realization that there was no turning back. The pleasure of pain was just too good.*

And Jay Lawrence understands, too. In her sizzling summertime story "Provocation," she explains: *It hurt like hell but it was a good kind of pain, one I needed to feel.*

Finally, Nikki Magennis sums the concept up eloquently: *Zen and the art of fucking. The way he empties the world and recreates it, perfect clarity and knowledge. Everything reduced to the places where our skin touches, or the places where he's marked me.…With the pain and the bliss melding under my skin, everything becomes clear.*

Hold my hand, and I'll take you with me. On a twisted, topsy-turvy journey through the various kinks and fetishes in this pleasure-meets-pain collection.

With no apologies,
Alison Tyler

THE SOUND OF ONE HAND CLAPPING

Nikki Magennis

C lear moments don't come by very often," he says, and as he
paces across the floor I think I know what he means. He is
walking toward me, after all, or away from me, backwards, and
the glimmer of light in the sky means it must be dusk, or early
morning.

I light a cigarette. That much is true. My hand is shaking, I
think, or it might be a mild hallucination. Visual disturbance to
add to all the other disturbed functions.

He has this effect on me, of blurring the days, smudging
the edges, like tightrope walking in zero gravity. I zoom. Up or
down, I don't know.

I pour another glass. It's dark and shining, the drink, could
be wine. Must be wine. Didn't we buy this only last week? Or
did I steal it somehow, lift it absentmindedly from a shelf in
the shop that's so bright-lit it makes me dizzy? I try to recall
where I found it. There was the scuffed yellow floor and the
metal shelving and the labels, loud and certain, so many labels.

Pictures of chickens and mountains. The radio playing far too loud. My hand in my pocket, the coins hot in my palm.

My memory shifts. He is beside me now, lying across the bed, a diagonal, a loose arrow pointing in many directions at once. His fingers, tangled in my hair, say *north,* and his eyes, jittery over in the direction of the door, say *south*, and his cock, laying long and limp across his thigh, says *stay right here.*

"Stay exactly where you are." Are those words in my mouth or my ear? I'm laughing. Someone's laughing. My throat burns from wine and laughter, and I light another cigarette to push out the burning. The room clouds. His hand drags down, catches in my mouth, pulls at my lip. I taste the tip of his fingers—metal. Stone. Ash.

When I suck on them, the blood in my mouth or his hand warms and everything turns a little orange. I run my tongue over his fingers like I'm playing piano. I want his whole fist in my mouth, suddenly.

I spit out his fingers, reach for the wineglass, swallow what's left. Then I hear the music again; it's been playing for an hour but melted into silence or what could pass for silence. I hear a line:

Drink to me only with thine eyes
And I will pledge with mine

It repeats. I let my head fall back, my eyes close. The image of the room is still there, a skeleton etched on the inside of my eyelids. The bedframe, the window, the blinds. The veranda outside. The balcony, eight floors up. The wind blowing in, blustering the curtains. We're in a Parisian dream. Insects scuttle over the floor, and there's a forty-watt bulb hanging from the ceiling. His skin is what I think they call swarthy, dark and rough on his face, melting to café au lait on his inner arms, his thighs, his belly. He wears a signet ring, in thick soft gold, on his pinky. His teeth are crooked, and he lies splayed across the sheets like a dirty banquet. I lean in to him.

I get lost in a sticky dream, my hands in his hair, our mouths eating each other, his knee splitting my thighs open, pushing, firm, sharp.

"Your bones are digging in."

A pillow is folded, pushed underneath my hips. We shift position. There's the sound of wet skin, the suck and the clicks. We're just kissing, winding our tongues around each other's, but our bodies are undulating too against each other, like we're trying to dance in a small space. We're astronauts. Houdinis.

"You wriggle too much."

"Yeah?"

"Yeah. Eager little hussy, aren't you?"

"Yep."

His eyebrows rise.

"That can be fixed, you know."

"With what?"

We're on our bellies, under the bed, fighting through the suitcases and boxes like we're soldiers crawling through some foreign jungle, our chins in the mud and the air full of strange smells. A hot night. Predators. Tunnels and trapdoors.

"This'll do," he says, and holds up a handful of silk scarves, the ones I've collected from Spain, from Japan, from parcels wrapped in tissue that accumulated round the bed like flowers in a hospital ward.

We slide out and struggle up, balls of dust clinging to us, one on each side of the bed, and suddenly it's become a stage, an arena. An altar.

I climb up and let the moment shiver between us. Already

naked, I add another layer of nakedness, the cocked hip and the jutting breast, the aura of sex. My body knows this dance; my face slides into a smile automatically, and my eyes drift over him, as sweet as the devil. I could be irresistible or ridiculous; the line is still swaying slightly. The only option is to play along, to mock the game gently while sticking to the rules. I lick my lips, and the cheap trick seems to work. He's perking up already, I notice, his cock swinging side to side as he reaches for me.

He takes my wrist gently, as though I'm wounded already, and ties it to a corner. He's good. Quick. Maybe he was a sailor in a past life. A crooked boy scout. The binding's not tight, but there's no way I can get free. I stare up at the blank ceiling and the crack running across, a hairline fracture from the building settling into the sand it's built on. I think of earthquakes.

When both wrists are pulled away and locked above my head, I feel opened, reluctantly alive, as though I'm welcoming a strange new day regardless of whether I want the sun on my face or not. Prometheus waiting for the eagle. He anchors my feet next, fixes me in the shape of an X. A target. Obscene and perfect.

But no.

"Too easy," he says, unties me and flips me over, repeats the process so now I'm on my front, face pressed into the pillow. When I breathe, the air blows back hot on my face and the rest of me is cold, naked, intact. He bundles the pillow under me again, raises my hips in the air, and I'm bent at a silly angle. I'm a little uncomfortable, just a little, but this time there's a pattern in the air, and instead of the fog I smell something different. Some electric promise.

The first strike shocks me. Smart it is, and sudden. A clap, resounding, scalding my arse so beautifully that I smile inside, involuntarily.

The pain blooms, and he lets the pause extend. So I can

feel the heat and the buzz, the audience gasping after the murder in the final act. Also so I can feel the tension build, the storm humming in the air, grow thicker, primed. For the second blow.

Which falls like snowflakes, barely more than a gentle clap, a kiss of affection from his palm onto my flesh. It melts. The heat spreads. He works his fingers into my crack, digging then for something in the earth that he knows is there, a mole burrowing, silent, intent, clothed in velvet.

He knows precisely what it is when he withdraws his hands, leaves me propped and wanting across the bed with my wrists tugging at the silk and my hips twisting. I am parched earth, waiting for rain, waiting for the thunderclouds to darken the sky over me. He is the god of weather now, someone to worship and pray to. Hence I am prone, begging for favors.

Tu me manques, in French—"you are lacking in me"—or, translated, "I miss you." That's what I feel now as I wait, the exquisite lack of his touch. I can't smell his salt and gravy scent, or feel the dry rasp of his hand against me. I can't see his eyes darting over me, provoking me and making me squirm. Nothing but the breeze that torments me, Mistral hot and Arctic cold, the dull blank and sweet sheets beneath me and the warm tug of the silk gripping my wrists, my ankles. My body is a blank until he grants me confirmation, until he wakes me with a kiss.

He hit me, and it felt like a kiss.

"Please."

The clouts come all at once, after a long intake of breath, a battery of stinging blows peppered over my behind. His hand feels huge, all encompassing. Now he smacks repeatedly, with the relentless precision of a metronome, with a beat in between each that lets my heart swell and my lungs fill. I hear the clapping now, there's no music, just the sound of this, him teaching me what's right and wrong, what's black and white, the difference between him striking me and not touching me, the swing back and forth.

"Again," I whisper, "again," and he keeps going, smacking till we're white hot and my whole groin is swarming with the word *yes*, shocked and ready and blessedly tender.

Then he takes me, shoves between my legs and fucks the cobwebs out of me, opens up the channel that explains everything, finally, and brings himself as close to me as a man can get. To the hilt and back out again, a definite and thorough screwing, a certain action with a certain destiny, and we're working together toward the bang now, him cupping my reddened cheeks in his hands as he goes, laying his palms very softly over the sore and tingled skin, reminding me as we hurtle down toward the meaning of life that he is there to guide me.

Enlightenment from behind, I think it might be. Zen and the art of fucking. The way he empties the world and recreates it, perfect clarity and knowledge. Everything reduced to the places where our skin touches, or the places where he's marked me, stamped his approval on my hindquarters like bestowing a blessing. Around us, I can see the room in sharp relief. I know exactly what hour it is, how fast the seconds are passing, how deep his cock reaches inside me. I know from his insistent thrusts how it feels for two people to be joined. Locked together. The wine glass is empty on the table beside us and the breeze is as smooth and cold as china, sliding over my skin. Life falls into place. It's a battle and a game, one that we both stand to win.

Once we hit the right momentum, the pace picks up. I can feel him tighten inside me, feel the urgency build. We are soldiers again, moving steadily closer to the target. I push back against him as he churns into me. We brace our arms and thighs in perfect choreography, hitting each other with the determined hunger of lovers.

If I asked him a question now, there would be only one answer, one that repeats and means something more every time.

"Please," I say, and "Yes," he answers, holding onto me, my hips and the tender wound he's helped open, the wound that gapes and swallows and delights in the hand that strikes it, that is finally and certainly forgiven, taken, cauterized.

Now I see for sure where we are. Now with the pain and the bliss melding under my skin, everything becomes clear. I no longer need to ask any questions, because the answer is contained within the question. The seed of him is the arrow, the pulsing and aching of my cunt as it welcomes his cock is the arrow. We are pointing toward each other and beyond to nowhere. We are agreed at last to stay here, right where we are, fucking on the brink of beautiful.

STING

Jessica Lennox

'm no tattoo expert. I'm not a fanatic or even what most would consider an enthusiast. I admit I know almost nothing about tattoos except that they make me want to fuck, and they hurt like hell. I'm not in love with the hurt-like-hell part, but I do enjoy the effect they have on me.

I know people who enjoy the pain of a tattoo. I'm not one of them, but I do understand that there's something seductive about knowing the person sporting the tattoo had the balls to withstand the experience. I've listened to people describe the pain as something akin to a religious experience, or something as blissful as sex. I'll admit I look at these people as if they have three heads, because to me it's more akin to an irritating, constant bee sting, and it takes every bone in my body not to slap or kick the person holding the tattoo gun.

Most tattoo shops are busiest late at night, when people are in the mood to party, or drink, or do something crazy, or all the above. I arrived relatively early, so there were only a few people hanging around—waiting to be worked on, I assumed. Since I'd never been to this particular shop before, I walked around hoping I'd get a vibe from the place.

Usually, staring at people is frowned upon, but when it comes to tattoos, it's welcomed and appreciated, so I indulged myself and let my eyes wander from stranger to stranger, staring at the depictions of women, animals, insects, flags, and a variety of other images worthy enough to adorn their skin.

After several minutes of euphoric lusting, I brought myself back to reality and began browsing the walls of endless designs. A few images caught my eye, and I noticed all were drawn by the same person: Gia. I asked the girl at the counter if the artist was available. Lucky me! She had an opening in an hour. I browsed some of the other designs, then sat down, impatiently, grabbing a random magazine to pass the time.

Finally, Counter Girl announced Gia was ready and led me into the back area. As I followed her through the maze of hallways, I noticed that each room was private, complete with a closable door. Most shops I'd been to had curtains between booths, at best.

As we stepped into a room at the end of the hall, Gia was standing with her back to me, setting up a small table of instruments. I sat down in a plastic chair and observed that her arms and the back of her neck were adorned with gorgeous artwork. Since she was engrossed in her work, I took advantage to indulge and stare at her tattoos.

After what seemed like an eternity, she turned around, and I think I stopped breathing. Although I'd never been with a woman, I've always had a crushing attraction for bad girl/tattooed/goth-girl types—and this one was certainly a stunner. She had an angelic face, but her dark makeup gave her a mysterious, hard-edged look, and her short black hair was sexy in contrast to her pale skin. The fact that her halter top showed off her perfect breasts didn't bother me at all.

I didn't know what else to do other than sit there and admire her until she finally motioned for me to sit on the table.

"What can I do for you?"

"Fuck me until I pass out" came to mind, but I reminded myself of my purpose for being here and replied, "I really dig your artwork. I don't have a specific design in mind, though. Perhaps you can do something freestyle, along the lines of a tribal design."

She stood there and looked me up and down for a few seconds. I realized that she'd probably had a thousand clients who didn't know what the hell they wanted, and here I was—another one. I longed not to be lumped into that crowd. After a pause, she crossed her arms and said, "Well, I *could*, but it's better if you choose a design; that way there's no misunderstanding. Know what I mean?"

I nodded, catching the glint in her mouth and seeing that she had the tip of her tongue pierced with a small hoop through it. "I understand," I said. "I'd be willing to sign something just so we don't have any problem. I trust your artistic ability."

She laughed and said, "Well, there's no need for the signature. Let me just get a few specifics. Where do you want the tat?"

"Here," I said, touching the right side of my groin.

"I'll have to shave you." I could swear she smirked when she said that.

"I'm already shaved. Completely."

Her eyebrows shot upward, then she asked, "How big do you want it?"

Again, my brain was going to the gutter, but I kept it cool and replied, "About two inches around."

"Something like this?" She pulled a page from a book and

brought it over to me, showing me a tribal design encased in an octagon. As I studied the design, I couldn't help but look at her glorious cleavage, now mere inches from my face. It took all my willpower not to lean over and lick her, but I got myself together and told her that the design was perfect.

She stood and shut the door. "I'm going to need you to remove your shorts and panties."

"Okay," I said, in a shaky voice. Did I mention that I hate the sting of the needle? I was also having some weird conflict between that and feeling excited at the same time. Not to mention Gia's energy was full of sexuality, and her hands were soon going to be on my half-naked body.

As I undressed, she turned her back to me, fiddling with things on the table. When I had everything off from the waist down, I sat on the table, put my hands in my lap, and said, "I'm ready."

She turned around, allowing her gaze to travel over my bare legs. "Lie back. That'll keep the skin taut, and it'll make it easier for me to work on you."

Oh, I wanted her to work on me all right. I eased myself backward. The table was cushioned with padded leather and a disposable paper cover, so it was soft and comfortable. The reclined position allowed me to see what she was doing, although I wasn't sure I wanted to, given my fear of needles. As I tried to get my nerves under control, her voice startled me, causing me to jump slightly.

"I'm going to clean the area with alcohol. Sorry for the cold."

Even though she had warned me, I jumped when I felt the spray hit my skin. She placed her warm hand on my abdomen and said "Easy" in a low voice, and that turned my arousal up a notch. This is not the state I wanted to be in. I wanted to be relaxed, not anxious and aroused. I tried to focus on anything but her hand, which was so close to my pussy that I wanted to scream, and somewhere in the back of my mind, I secretly wanted her to touch me there. But she was all business and seemed not to notice anything out of the ordinary as she wiped my skin clean with a sterile gauze pad.

Then I heard the buzz of the gun, and all thoughts of anything sexual disappeared in an instant. I tried to calm myself by breathing slowly and thinking about warm, tropical places and sandy beaches. I reminded myself about how happy I'd be when this was all over. I would be sporting a gorgeous new tattoo. It was a nice idea, but I bit my lip anyway, bracing against the pain.

As Gia worked on me, she kept moving her hand to different areas on my body, trying to get the best angle. I felt her fingers move from my abdomen, to my thigh, to my hip, and although I know she didn't do this for any purpose other than her work, it was turning me on like crazy. I tried to use this as a distraction from the pain. I pulled my focus together, thinking only of her hand. No more thoughts of that annoying sting that kept biting me. Although my arousal was intensifying, I kept reminding myself that her touch was not for this purpose. But when she placed her hand just above my pussy to pull the skin taut, I couldn't help but moan and arch my hips slightly. She looked up at me then and said, "Everything okay?"

I could feel my cheeks turning red, as I answered, "Yes, sorry."

She smiled and said, "If you need a break, just let me know. Otherwise, I really need you to keep still."

She had no idea how difficult that was proving to be, but I nodded anyway and forced myself to relax. I closed my eyes and concentrated on my breathing, keeping my inhales and exhales steady and even, trying to forget the now insistent throb in my pussy.

As I began to finally reach a state of calm, her voice brought me slamming back to the present when she said, "You're wet."

My eyes flew open and I looked at her while she stared into my eyes, and then glanced down at my center of arousal. I was so embarrassed I didn't know what to say, so I didn't say anything. Instead, I lay there mortified, my face turning fifteen shades of red.

"Do you like the sting of the needle?" she asked, running her finger lightly between my pussy lips. "Is that why you're so wet?"

I shook my head no, still unable to speak.

"You could have fooled me," she said as she dipped her finger in and pressed lightly on my clit.

"Oh fuck," I moaned, finding my voice and arching my hips toward her.

She put the tattoo gun down and ran her hands slowly upward, over my stomach, then back down over my thighs. "You have great skin," she said, pushing my legs apart. Her voice was like liquid silk; I could have listened to it all day. I gladly let her spread my legs. "That's it, let me open you up," she said, using her fingers to part my swollen lips. At first, I thought I was going to come just from watching her touch me, but when she leaned down and let the tip of her tongue glide over my pussy, I felt as though I was going to pass out.

As I lay there moaning and panting, I suddenly wondered if anyone else could hear me. Realizing they probably could, I tried to be quiet, but when she eased two fingers into my cunt, I gasped and moaned even louder.

"Sh," she said, coaxing me to be quiet as she continued to trace my clit with her tongue. Her touch was so light, I thrust upward to try to get more, but she said, "If you don't stop that, I'm going to spank you."

I looked at her with an amused smile, but honestly I couldn't tell if she was serious or kidding. I thrust upward once more, and she surprised me by giving my pussy a quick, stinging slap.

I was so shocked I didn't know what to do. I lay there rigid and unsure of whether to give in to my arousal or get the hell out of there as fast as I could. No, it was too soon to give up, I decided. I wanted to see where she was going to take me.

"Yes, Ma'am," I answered, hoping that would signal to her that I wanted to continue.

"Good girl," she said as she continued to play for several glorious minutes, her fingers in my cunt and her tongue on my clit.

"You're so wet," she said. "If I didn't know better, I'd swear that you do like the sting. Perhaps not from the needle but from something more intimate, like my hand. What do you think? Should we experiment a little?"

I whimpered, not sure which way to go, but she made my mind up for me by giving my pussy a little tap. That didn't hurt at all. In fact, the pressure felt pretty good, if only for a moment. I wanted more and started to thrust upward, but then remembered she didn't like that and quickly stopped myself.

"Ah, you're learning. That's very good."

She continued to administer quick slaps, a little harder each time and with a little more frequency. The more she spanked my pussy, the more aroused I got, and eventually I didn't even mind that the slaps were getting harder. Finally, I couldn't control my body anymore, I had to move. I started thrusting my hips gently in time with her hand, and she let me. At one point she pushed my legs apart, and the effect of her bare-hand spanking my open pussy was almost too much to take. Each time her hand came down on me, she hesitated momentarily, keeping her hand there, putting pressure on my clit for a prolonged moment. I knew it was only a matter of seconds and I wouldn't be able to hold off any longer. Then she bent down and bit my clit gently, pulling with her teeth, and that was all I could take. I gripped the table, clenched my jaw shut, and came in her mouth while three of her fingers deliciously fucked me.

I collapsed against the table, exhausted. After a few moments, I forced my eyes to focus and looked at her with a mixture of relief and surprise.

She winked at me and said, "Welcome back. That was amazing, but I need to finish you off now."

I gave a short laugh and said, "I think you just did."

"No, I mean your tattoo. It isn't finished yet."

"Oh, yeah," I replied, suddenly aware that I wasn't feeling any pain.

NO SUBSTITUTE FOR EXPERIENCE

James Walton Langolf

R yan doesn't realize how much he wants to hurt Julia until she lays the strap across his palm.

"It's okay," she says. "I want you to."

Even then he is thinking about his mother, the stern look on her face when he'd step out of line. She didn't have to lay a hand on him. The look was enough.

Julia has a look, too. This one thrown back over her shoulder, casual as a pinch of salt for luck. Ryan can almost meet her eyes.

"I can't," he answers, but he knows it isn't true.

She takes the trailing end of the belt and brushes the leather against his cheek.

"Why do you keep coming here?" she asks.

He feels his cock throbbing against the zipper of his jeans, and he can't suppress a grin. "Is that a trick question?"

A flick of her wrist and the belt snaps against his skin. He cries out, more in surprise than pain. "Jesus, Julia. What do you want me to say?"

It's always this way with her. He never knows the rules. Sometimes she doesn't speak to him at all, fixes her gaze on a point somewhere over his shoulder while she writhes on the floor. On these days he wonders if maybe he's a ghost. Maybe she's been touching him all along, but her hands just slip right on through with nothing to connect to. All he needs now are some chains to rattle, or maybe he's already wearing those, too.

"Nothing," she says. The belt drops from her hands, useless at her feet. She turns toward the window. The blinds are up, and the field behind her house is drifted white. The sun is setting, and the honey-colored light reflected off the snow turns her bare skin to gold. She cocks her head to the side as if listening to the sound of the icicles melting from the roof, and the angle of her neck seems to draw his teeth. He sets his jaw and waits for her to speak again.

Her curly black hair is cropped short, leaving her skin naked and vulnerable. Tattoo vines snake across the small of her back, blood dripping from the thorns. Ryan moves to touch her but stops before he reaches her skin. He wonders what it would feel like. Her actual flesh. Would it be warm? Smooth? Like silk laid out in the sun? Or cool and hard like pearls at the deep dark bottom of the sea where the sunlight never penetrates.

"Julia," he says, and his voice scrapes in his throat.

She won't turn back to face him, and still he doesn't understand her. Doesn't understand himself. Ryan is only nineteen and she's older. Maybe forty. Maybe a year or two younger and just tired, but she carries it well.

When Julia asked him why he was here, he'd laughed, but it's a valid question.

She'd come into the store nearly a month ago. He remembers it was slow, the summer people long gone. There hadn't been a customer all night. Her short denim skirt was frayed at the hem, and her top was made of some filmy purple fabric that looked like a silk scarf tied at the back of her neck.

She wore too much lipstick and mascara, and both were smeared prettily on her freckled cheeks. Wrinkles deep as scars creased the corners of her eyes when she smiled. Her hair was snarled and tangled like she'd just rolled out of bed. Ryan imagined her sheets still wet.

He watched her move through the store, aimless but graceful, like she'd forgotten what she'd come in for but knew she'd remember when she saw it. Then she turned and stretched to reach a bottle of tequila on a shelf above her head, and Ryan saw the red stripes running up the back of her legs, peeking from under her shirt as the fabric rode up on her back.

She'd heard his sudden inhalation.

"A hickory switch," she'd said, and he couldn't even answer, just stood there and gaped. Julia got her bottle, twisted off the top, and drank deep. It wasn't allowed and she hadn't paid, but Ryan didn't say anything.

It was late and he needed to close up, but Julia didn't leave. She'd followed him around the store as he straightened shelves and swept, as he mopped, watching him with eyes so dark blue they were nearly violet.

They must have talked some, but he couldn't remember what they said.

She'd sat on the counter with her ankles crossed while he counted out his drawer. The finger-shaped bruises on her thighs distracted him so he had to count the dimes twice.

"Do you want to know why?" Julia had asked. Her bones looked fragile as spun sugar. She was the kind of woman anyone would want to protect.

Ryan had said no, but he was already nodding his head. He'd

flushed a deep and searing red. Julia had laughed out loud, and Ryan felt the sound inside his skin like the rushing of his own blood. That was when her fingers found his belt. He wanted to stop her, but he was afraid if he touched her, he'd be the one to break.

"Wait," he'd said.

"Have you ever?" was how she'd answered, her thumbs through his loops.

"No."

She'd laughed again, and this time her mockery gave the sound rough texture and sharp edges. His fingers, clenched into fists, were already starting to ache.

She hadn't even told him her name yet, and already he wanted to shatter her just to see her put back together again. She was excited too. He could hear it in her voice, see the way her skin had flushed, the way her nipples thrust against the thin fabric of her shirt.

Ryan had taken a step toward her and Julia had stepped back, hands up, palms out—in defense or surrender he couldn't be sure. Her eyes still laughed at him.

"Easy, baby boy," she'd said, trying to draw blood.

The beer sign lights flashed on and off across her skin as she'd dropped to her knees. The buckled linoleum must have dug into her, but she'd looked up at him, eyes wide, mouth just open.

She'd untied her top at the neck and let it fall. Silver rings ran through each dark pink nipple. The flesh around them was raw and red. Ryan swayed on his feet, and she'd slipped her two little fingers through the hoops and tugged.

"You like that?" Julia had asked.

He'd said nothing and she'd pulled harder, stretching the skin tight and white and shiny. The expression on her face, something like prayer, something painted in watercolor, sketched in charcoal. She was that beautiful.

She'd rocked back and forth on her heels, tugging her nipples. A tiny pink wedge of tongue poked from one corner of her mouth as she made a noise deep in her throat like something caught and desperate. Still, it was her eyes that had held him in place.

"Stop. Stop. Please, lady. You have to stop."

But still he was rubbing his cock through his jeans. His skin was tight and chafed raw, burning inside and out.

Her rocking had sped up; her motion and moaning grew more frenzied until finally she'd closed those amazing violet eyes, thrown back her head, and howled. The sound had hit the back of his skull cold and hard as chunks of hail.

She'd held herself motionless for a space of breaths, if either of them had actually been breathing. Then she'd stood once more, smoothed her skirt, straightened and tied her shirt. The flush on her throat and cheeks was the color of fresh-crushed strawberries. Her freckles stood out like tiny brands, and she leaned in close so he could smell the sex and soap on her skin.

"Thank you," she'd whispered against his neck before she turned toward the door.

"Wait!" he'd cried. "What about me?"

"You want to know how it feels?"

His ridiculous cock had strained at the front of his pants, a small dark spot growing where the pre-come had started to bleed through. He'd felt his pulse beating there and inside his head.

He'd have got down on his knees and begged her—for what, he couldn't say. And it didn't matter because she had just shaken her head, kissed the air around his cheek, and walked away.

Now she comes back night after night like a haunt to tease and torment him. Always a fresh bruise. Always he is too afraid to ask her how or who. She puts on her little performances, exhibiting her addiction, or is it his? And how can he ever be sure?

He makes his promises, and he locks the door at closing time. Then Julia shows up on the other side of the rain-streaked glass, and he just can't turn her away.

His desire has weight now. Length and breadth. Scales, claws, and teeth. It terrifies and exalts him. Her shame makes him feel debased.

She gets herself off on the store counter, in every dusty aisle, in the back seat of his car, on the hood of hers, back at her place the time she flagellated herself with a cat-o'-nine tails until the skin broke and tiny drops of blood speckled the sheets like runes. He wanted to read his future there.

Still, Julia never allows him to lay a hand on her. Her broken flesh is something sacred and forbidden. The things she shows him make him feel low and mean. Jesus, he thinks, what am I becoming? What have I become already?

It's her blood, but he's the sacrifice.

Always she asks him if he wants her to tell him how it feels. He does, but she never will.

Julia is smiling now, her watercolor smile, and Ryan feels himself coming undone.

He should be begging her forgiveness; instead he's feeling for the strap. He wants to kneel there by the bed, crawl across the floor, but his own wanting is weighing him down. His weakness only feeds his rage. He's getting a hold of it now—or it is taking hold of him?—either way somebody's going to bleed.

"Lay your ass down," somebody says. The voice is Ryan's.

"Yes."

Julia stretches out on the bed, her cheek on the pillow, watching him so serenely, eyes full of trust he knows he doesn't deserve. With one finger he traces the ridges of her spine.

He feels a shudder and has no way of knowing which of them trembles.

The sound of his open palm against her ass is not as loud as he had thought it would be, but the weight of it brings his teeth together on his tongue. The taste of blood fills his mouth.

"This is me," he says.

"Yes."

He smacks her again.

"Can you feel it?"

"Yes."

Again and the red shapes of his fingers stand out clearly on her skin.

"Can you?"

"Yes."

She rolls over onto her back, her legs spread apart. Her hands shake as she fumbles with his fly.

He kisses the hollow of her throat, and she says "Yes" one last time as he slips inside. He moves slowly even though she's pressing up hard against him.

There's a lot of pain here, more than a little rage, but he feels such a sense of peace pounding himself into her. The damp heat of her, the hungry animal scent of her, crushes the breath out of him, sets his severed nerves aflame. Sweat makes them both slippery, and still he's holding onto her shoulders pushing himself higher, deeper into her. He's made contact, made himself known, and he won't break now.

The heat is rolling off her like a fever dream. She's pulling at his hair. "I can't," he says. She doesn't answer but digs her heels into the bony part of his ass.

He's making some noise now. He may be trying to speak her name. He isn't sure.

There are lights behind his eyes and a vibration inside his

skin that's a little like being torn apart, a little more like being born.

Then something's coming loose, something's breaking free, and he's telling her, "Take it, take it, take it honey. Take it all, you bitch."

And she does.

Finally, stillness—outside and inside his skin. No movement or sound but blood through veins, his and hers the same.

"Tell me," Julia says. "Tell me how it feels."

PANTY LINES

Sommer Marsden

When I answer the phone, he says, "Put them on."

That's all. Then he hangs up.

I put them on.

Four hours later, I meet Steve for dinner. Our favorite place. A nice candlelit dinner to celebrate the end of the workweek. I listen to my heels tapping on the parking lot to try to distract myself. Anything to pull me from the bizarre mix of arousal, excitement, and pain coursing through me. It hurts to walk. Every step torture. Every flex of my muscles a searing pain.

He is watching my face. After playing this game for awhile now, I know what he is looking for. The wince when I sit, the shifting in my seat, the way my hands move to offer myself some relief and then still in my lap because I know that's forbidden.

"How do you feel?" he asks and pours me a glass of red wine from the table.

I don't sip like a lady. I take a big swig. I have also learned that getting that first glass of wine or that first shot of tequila in

me will lessen the pain. Turn it from glass shards on my skin to
a dull burning pain. A little more manageable.

"Like I might go insane," I sigh and take a more demure sip
of my drink.

"How wet are you?" he asks in his normal tone. He does not
lower his voice or lean in so only I can hear. He simply asks me
as if he is asking if I've had my oil changed lately.

I squirm a little, as I always do at the question and how bold
he is. The simple act of asking makes me that much wetter.
I can feel the moisture in my panties as I shift. My too-tight
panties. The ones he makes me wear for our special occasions.
They leave deep red lines in my skin. They are torturous. but I
am always rewarded. And the pain is a welcome thing for me.
Dancing with the monster. The pain makes what comes later that
much sweeter. We discovered this by accident, and now it has
become ritual.

Hour one is annoying.

Hour two I am tender.

Hour three and it's maddening.

Hour four and I have hit the point where I want it to end. I
know this from experience. We are only in hour one.

"Very wet," I sigh and sip again. The waiter will arrive soon.
Steve has already ordered for us as he always does. Surf and
Turf, a nice red wine, and cheesecake for dessert. Every item
on our menu a hoop I must jump through to get my reward. To
get home and get my too-tight panties peeled off and my needs
taken care of.

"Size?" he asks as the waiter puts our small salads on the
table.

I pop a cherry tomato in my mouth and chew, though my
increasing discomfort has stolen my appetite. I can't get up and
move around. I cannot find a new position and shift here, there,

and everywhere. I must sit and focus on him and eat my meal and act as if all is well. More moisture seeps into the crotch of my cotton bondage.

"Two," I say, playing along.

"And you, Janelle, wear what size?"

I want to sigh because he knows damn well what size I wear. But the look in his eyes lets me know that his cock is hard. Very hard and waiting for me. I must jump through the hoop.

"An eight."

Three sizes too small, shrunken in the dryer by my husband on purpose. My key to sexual bliss.

It started when Steve's sister Marie came to stay for the weekend. Marie's laundry had gotten mixed in with ours, and somehow a pair of her panties ended up in my drawer. I am tall and lean but have a healthy ass. Marie is small and light-weight and has the flattest ass on planet earth. When I put her panties on by mistake, I had been rushing out the door. Through a meeting and lunch and the rest of my workday, I suffered. I had worn a short skirt that day, and flashing my ass to the office would have gotten me fired, so I suffered. For nine hours. In Marie's panties. Steve was there when I got home and took them off. Red indentations and chafing marks all over my skin. When he ran his fingers along my skin to trace them, I gasped. Jumped. Shuddered.

When he fucked me right after that, I did all the same things.

The pain and the pleasure were married that night.

Marie eventually called for her missing items. But Steve went right out and bought an identical pair. In Marie's size. And then, to add insult to injury, or in this case, pleasure to pain—he washed them in hot water and then dried them. The pair I am currently wearing are even smaller than the pair that started this whole thing.

"Eat your salad," he says. I do. Each bite tastes worse than the one before. Each chewing session does nothing to shift my focus from the burning bite of elastic into the tops of my thighs, the swell of my asscheeks, the cleft between my thighs. My attention is focused solely on my discomfort no matter what I try. But my mind also supplies vivid images of my eventual release, and my pussy floods the tiny torturous panties. There's nothing I can do but squirm.

"And sit still," Steve adds sternly.

So I do.

The final hour of dinner lasts a lifetime. Or feels like it. I am now completely obsessed both with the urge to shift and the voice in my head that reminds me that I cannot. As always, Steve has the rest of my dinner wrapped up for me to take. I never manage to eat much on these nights out. I have, however, downed three glasses of wine. I know he's aware of what I'm doing, but he lets me. I can only assume he doesn't want me to suffer in an uncontrolled way. That wine gives me a little sense of relief and control, though this is pretty much an illusion and we both know it.

"Take the back way home." He kisses me and heads off to his car.

I walk the agonizing walk to my car and hiss as I sit in the low bucket seat. I start the engine and drive the back way to our house. The back way takes fifteen minutes longer than the straight shot down a main road. More time in the panties. More torture. More anticipation. Wetter panties. I can feel my own liquids seeping down my inner thighs as I pick my way painfully up the front walk.

The door is open and Steve is inside. Waiting for me. I move a little faster now because I know that soon, I will be able to breathe. I move a little faster because I know it will get a little

worse before it gets a lot better. But that's okay. I can handle it.
Need it, if I'm honest.

"Upstairs, Janelle!" he calls when the door shuts behind me.
I climb the stairs slowly. Each step makes me wince.

He's waiting in the bedroom. Naked cock standing straight
out. He watches me enter. Pins me with that gaze. His fist jerks
up and over the shaft a few times, and I clench my thighs at the
sight. His hand on his cock never fails to make me crazy. I'm
feeling more than a little crazy as it is.

"Take off your dress," he commands. I move automatically,
without question or thought. I reach around, unzip my dress,
and let it fall to the floor.

Steve nods and jerks his fist again. The smooth head of his
cock is turning the most magical shade of violet. "Bra."

I unhook and let the flimsy bit of lingerie fall to the floor.
Now it is just me and the too-tight panties. Steve motions me
forward with his hand, and I go. My inner thighs are nearly raw
from the lack of circulation and chafing. I would give my right
arm for an ice pack and a shot of whiskey.

"Lay down and let's see how bad off you are." I lie on the
bed and let him do his examination. I shoot glances at his hard-
on as he begins to look me over. He yanks the elastic, pulling it
harder into my indented flesh as I try not to cry. His cock jerks
when he does this, as if an invisible string of arousal is tied to it.
He works his way around the leg openings, tugging the elastic
hard as I try not to beg him to stop. Every time he tugs, his cock
jumps in response. He pulls hard on the low waistband, and it
bites into the raw line of skin along my lower belly. Finally, he
yanks up and the too-tight crotch pulls flush and splits wide my
lower lips. I bite my tongue to keep from crying.

"Pretty sore, I imagine," he says softly. Speaking more to
himself than to me. "On your belly."

I turn and close my eyes. Try to breathe. Wait. The first blow hits right where the leg hole has rubbed my asscheek red. The pain is nearly overwhelming, but the aftershock of pleasure that ripples through my flesh and deep inside my cunt makes it bearable. The other cheek takes its turn, as does the flesh of my lower back. My eyes are leaking salty tears, but a steady beat has started between my thighs. When I don't think I can stand anymore, he traces the afflicted areas with his gentle palms and tongue. Alternating between the two. Always keeping me off balance.

Finally, I can take a deep breath when he says, "Let's get you out of these." He begins to peel the wet, tiny panties from my body. I am not allowed to move or shift to help him. I must stay perfectly still and let him do the removal alone. Sometimes the biting pain on the deeply dented skin is enough to make me scream. I don't scream.

The horrid panties are finally off. They are off and his hot tongue is back on me. Licking along the wounded skin, following the trail of pain. I sob just a little into the pillow from the pleasure. He turns me again, licking along the red, red lines as he shoves a finger deep into me. Finding the swollen bundle of my G-spot and pulsing his fingertip in a perfect rhythm.

I come. This time I sob deeply. I sound like a wounded animal.

He pushes another big finger into me as his mouth finds my clit. So sensitive and ready it almost hurts when he brushes his flattened tongue against me. He flexes both fingers, licks my sore inner thighs, and returns his tongue.

I come for the second time. This time I am babbling. I think I'm saying, "Please, please, please…" I could be wrong.

The blood flow returning to the wicked marks left by nothing more than elastic and cotton is a tingling, electric bliss. He

pushes two pillows under my belly, raising my ass high. I hear
the dresser drawer, feel him kneeling behind me. He pushes into
my cunt. His cock so hard I feel like I'm dying. He runs his
fingertips along my marks and grunts approvingly. I'm so wet, I
fear he might fall out when he pulls back before thrusting into
me again. I don't lose him, but he's hitting all the right places
and his fingers on my wounds are heaven.

My cunt bunches around him. Another orgasm to come, we
both know. I hear the wet sounds of a lube bottle, feel the cool
liquid against my asshole. He's pounding into me now, his fingers
dancing over my lines every so often. When I feel the crown of
the dildo nudge my ass, I push back. I'm ready. No preamble.

He slides it into me. He slides into me. Two cocks. Two
entries. At some point, he briefly takes both hands along the
now fading dents in my skin. It feels like he's painting me.

"Feel better?" he asks and I nod, waiting.

He resumes his rhythm and pushes me up over that edge one
more time, and this time he comes with me.

LUCKY

N. T. Morley

Excuse me, Mistress, may I lick your pussy?"

Claire was up with her ass in the air bent halfway over the bar; thank God the barstools were so fucking sturdy at this place or she'd have gone headfirst into a wall of premium vodkas. She'd climbed up halfway onto the bar not to pull a Coyote Ugly but to get the attention of the bartender, Dylan, who was completely engrossed in flirting with a cute boy in a sailor suit.

Claire came down from the barstool and settled into her six-inch stiletto heels, disbelief and anger evident on her pale face. What the fuck had he just said?

The six-foot, jockey-clad male submissive who stood before her was lucky —very, very lucky—that Claire had been trying for a full ten minutes to get the attention of Dylan. The submissive was also very lucky that he had such an amazingly nice chest.

The expression of shock and outrage that passed over Mistress Claire's face was actually a cover-up for the aesthetic pleasure she took in looking at the guy. Besides the chest, he had a nice pair of muscular tattooed arms and... my word. Claire popped her eyes back up to his, and made them hard, inspired by the front of his jockey shorts. My, how she did love tighty-whiteys.

"What did you say?" she hissed with practiced outrage.

The submissive dropped his eyes and lowered himself to one knee. "I asked if I could lick your pussy, Mistress," he said. "I know it's rude. I'm so sorry. But I've been trying to catch your attention for an hour—"

"Did I give you permission to kneel?"

The submissive's mouth hung open for an instant, and he said "I apologize for—" as he began to stand.

"Did I give you permission to stand?" Claire spat.

The submissive stood there tottering in mid-crouch, unsure what to do. She let him hover there for a moment, taking pleasure in his insecurity. When his eyes raised to Claire's to beg direction before his impressive thigh muscles gave way, she snapped "Did I give you permission to look at me?" and he went back to one knee, shaking his head.

"Do you honestly think that cunnilingus involves licking pussy?"

He shook his head rapidly.

"What does a little bitch like you lick, then?" She cut him off when he opened his mouth, by hissing "One word!"

"Clit," he murmured. "Mistress."

Which, seriously, was the only right answer; if he'd said anything else, he would have been kneeling in front of an empty barstool, and the next day Claire would have been complaining to her friends about how fucking clueless guys were. The fact that he'd actually said two words, Claire totally let slide.

Claire stuck her foot out and poked the front of his tighty-whiteys with her pointy toe. She was somewhat dismayed to discover that her read on the guy a moment ago had been wrong; he had not, in fact, been hard. He was now, though, hard enough that the jock strap could not contain him, and he was definitely breaking the rules by letting his swelling dickhead poke out over the waistband.

"Did I tell you to put that away?" growled Claire as he reached for his cock to shuffle it back into his underwear. He looked cowed and put his hands at his sides while she planted her butt on the barstool and teased his cockhead with the bottom of her shoe. She continued to tease it with one stiletto heel and smiled as he squirmed.

"What kind of a man asks that of a strange woman at a bar?" she asked. "Without introducing himself."

He opened his mouth to speak, and she snapped, "Did I tell you to introduce yourself?" His face went red and he fell silent. She laughed and his cock swelled under the assault of her stiletto heel and her contempt. She could feel herself swelling, too, her clit engorging against the mesh G-string. She hooked the front of his jockeys with her heel and pulled them down to his balls, tucking them under and taking a moment to scrape the stiletto under them, forcing the tightly cinched orbs on the far side of his waistband, leaving his cock pointing out invitingly and, more importantly, with staggering vulnerability.

Claire was kind of amazed she'd pulled it off; six weeks ago, she'd barely been able to walk in high heels; now she was performing complicated cock and ball torture moves with stiletto heels, all while feeling her heart pound with swiftly mounting arousal.

Every few seconds, she glanced around for bar monitors; they were not supposed to be playing here, which was just one of the many things that made her so wet.

She planted her stilettos on either side of him, leaning forward both to shroud his exposed cock from any potential narcs nearby and to give him a look up her skirt, which did not react modestly to being on a barstool. In fact, the look on his face told Claire that he could see just about everything.

"Speak," she said.

He did not say anything. "I can't hear you," she growled.

"I'm sorry, Mistress," said the submissive. "I've... I've been watching you, and I wanted—"

"You already said what you wanted," Claire cut him off, taking great pleasure in it. "And I'm considering the offer, but I can't let a pickup line like that go unpunished. If I'm going to even consider it, first I'm going to have to make you pay for being rude."

"Of course, Mistress," said the submissive. "I—I'd—I'd like that."

She leaned forward, chuckling, and caressed his face, from hair to temple to cheek to throat and then hard with her thumb into his mouth, deep, forcing his tongue down, which made him whimper.

"I don't think you will," said Claire, and he went hot-red from face to chest to cock. He obediently sucked her thumb while she dug her nails firmly into the flesh of his throat. He whimpered some more when she pushed her thumb far enough back.

Oh motherfucking holy Hell she got hot when he whimpered and gagged like that. It was like a hot wave of angry need from her sex to the back of her throat. She'd been performing her final test of the courtship ritual—five o'clock shadow test; if the fucker was anything less than baby smooth it would be a flogging at best, maybe a caning—no way Claire was going home with razor burn on a friggin' Tuesday. Her fingers had caressed a face like silk or satin, but her thumb had found a tongue as warm and wet and supple as they came, with one added feature that would have been the deal closer if she wasn't already sold: a tongue stud, smooth and flat and heavy.

She had her hand out of his mouth in an instant, was off the barstool and had her skirt up and her panties down, giving him (and anyone else in the bar who was looking) a glimpse of her smooth sex. Then she'd stepped out of her panties and spread her legs, which made her skirt crawl up and put her smooth, exposed sex right at face level. She bent close, caressing his face some more; she liked her clit so much better without the fucking mesh. "You want a taste of this?"

He knew, as she did, that they weren't supposed to play at the bar; but on a Tuesday, anything might happen, especially since Dylan was making out with his sailor boy instead of getting drinks or monitoring the bar area. It was evident from the way his eyes went bright and hungry, the way his mouth hung slack, that he was ready and eager to eat Claire's perfect pussy; the way his tongue lolled out when she hooked one leg over his shoulder and began to pull him closer told her everything she needed to know. Which was what gave her such perverse pleasure in planting her other knee against his shoulder. She held him well out of reach but close enough to smell her, a fact attested to by the long, deep breaths he was taking.

Claire had never been much for toys, really; she liked hands and claws and teeth most of all. But her ex-boyfriend Steve had purchased her the most wicked little toy, pleading the twin male prerogatives of being concerned about her well-being and wanting to know she could beat him up. She kept it tucked at the top of her right boot, lacing that side slightly looser. She snapped open the expanding baton and watched him go pale.

"What's that?" blurted the submissive.

She caressed his face with it. She tried to surreptitiously

glance around to see if any bar staff were watching, but truth is she didn't care anymore; the fact that these things were illegal in this state only made her wetter, knowing she was going to apply it to this cheeky stranger's ass.

"This is your punishment," she cooed, bending close to him, moving her legs to envelop him and letting her smooth thighs caress the sides of his face as she coaxed him closer. He grabbed the struts of the barstool and hung on for dear life. As she leaned forward, her breasts popped out of her corset, and she grabbed the back of his hair to force his head back. She began to draw a circle around his face with one hard nipple, then the other, while she looked down into his face and savored the fear. "You want me to punish you, don't you?" she asked in a voice as rich as chocolate. "After all, I don't even know you and you asked me if you could suck my pussy. That's very rude, isn't it? I should punish you for it, shouldn't I? That's what you want, isn't it?"

He swallowed hard; his eyes flickered to the baton, and she held his head against her belly as she reached down to prod his balls with it.

"Say 'Please punish me, Mistress,'" she purred, and oh, how guilty she should have felt that it was the reluctance she hoped for in his voice that made her so fucking wet. But she didn't feel guilty, just horny, and once she heard him say it, his words hesitant and trembling, she pulled him close, pinning his face against her breasts and his body between her thighs. She leaned down, discovering that with a tall guy like this, the baton barely reached where she wanted it to.

"Pull down your panties, bitch," she purred. "Show me what I'm hurting."

She'd been a bit worried he'd change his mind, but then, it was that possibility that excited her. Though he didn't. He pulled his jockey shorts down to mid-thigh, exposing an ass so perfect she desperately wished she could see it better. But it was worth it to have him pinned against her, surging and quivering, as she leaned over, reached the baton down and caressed his bubble butt.

Normally, she would have warmed him up, but how long did they have until they got kicked out of the bar? Not long, probably, so there was no time to fuck around.

She swatted. His body jumped against hers. She sighed with pleasure and struck him again. It really took some doing with a tool like the baton—hit even a muscular ass like this at the wrong angle and she could really hurt the little fucker. But hit him obliquely, with great care, and—oh, yes, that's the thing. She began swatting him regularly as he writhed and trembled in her grasp, his ass going red as she drew him closer. She picked up speed. He squirmed. He let out a pathetic little whimper. His cock made a clanging sound against the metal strut of the barstool. He jumped back from the impact. She swatted him again. His back arched; he gripped the barstool firmly and tried to suppress his cries as she punished his ass.

When he opened his mouth, she silenced him with her breast—if he really made some noise, he'd get the monitors over here from the dungeon, and nobody wanted that. Claire pulled his face hard against her, and he began to obediently pleasure her nipple with his mouth and tongue. "There, there, let Mama make it better," she cooed, and grabbed his hair to shove his face between her legs.

She almost lost it as she felt his tongue against her clit. It had been too fucking long since she'd had a guy down there; all this sadist and masochist shit had her totally distracted by hurting people, and most guys who offered to service her were less like eager little suck slaves and more like beard-burn nightmares drooling on her snatch. She'd been meaning to find the right submissive boy to properly train, but so far none of them had seemed worth the effort.

This time, she forgot all about the training; there were a few moments, sure, toward the beginning, when she was opening her mouth momentarily to give pointers, but each time all that came out was a girly sound of pleasure, so she stopped that right away. And before he'd started, she had it all planned out, how he was going to do a pathetic job, and she'd bend over and give him another ten or twenty hard smacks on the ass, getting hotter as she punished him until maybe she could even let him get her close.

That ended up not happening, because there was no beard-burn, there was just this…tongue, doing things that made her eyes roll back in her head. He did not dive right in to the clit; sure, she'd given him shit earlier about using the term "lick pussy," which would have been the perfect excuse to punish the poor fucker when he did exactly that—except that it felt good enough that she didn't want him to stop. There were long lush minutes of him teasing her from top to bottom, majora to minora, upper thigh to entrance, all tangled up beautifully with a little clit, a little more clit, still more clit, surging slowly as he built her to her breaking point.

Then he was on her clit, at exactly the right moment, when she couldn't stand waiting and didn't want any more teasing, just the slow steady surge of his tongue against her clit as she rocked back and forth on the barstool.

For Claire, there were two kinds of tongue jobs; the first was the familiar experience of being in the hands of a guy who could take direction and help her get off; that she knew, but it was exceedingly rare. Then there was this, which was pretty much entirely new; this guy seemed to know how to get her off himself, almost without her participation, which seemed disgustingly untoppy, but who really gave a fuck?

People were watching now, all around her, keeping a respectful distance—barely—as she crossed her legs behind his head and spread her arms out Christ-style to steady herself against the bar.

As his tongue seethed against her, she realized she was actually going to come, which simultaneously gave her a feeling of surrender and a thrill of overriding dominance—she had never done it before, not in this way, and she was as powerless as she was powerful, powerless to stop it and powerful enough to let it happen.

She came, pleasure coursing through her body. She writhed shamelessly, moaning evidently, grinding her hips up and down and fucking her pussy against his face, not caring that people were crowded tight around her and everyone in the bar seemed to be cheering. She'd popped all the way out of her corset, and she realized she was probably breaking about thirty liquor laws. But even Dylan had the grace to wait until she'd finished and had pushed the submissive's head out of her crotch before leaning over the bar and saying, "Claire, do you and Shawn mind taking it to the play space?"

Her eyes took a moment to focus; the submissive knelt before her, panting, his cock still sticking out hard and his face glistening with drool and her juices.

Claire laughed, looked at Dylan, looked at the no longer nameless submissive, and said "Yeah, or maybe my apartment."

Dylan spread his hands in good-natured surrender. "Girlfriend, that's up to you."

She knew she was fairly insane for even considering it, but the guy really had a way with that tongue.

Claire eyed the sub, whose name was apparently Shawn. She raised one eyebrow, read the expression on his face. She squared herself on the barstool and nudged his cock with the tip of her boot. It was harder than ever.

She bent forward and caressed his face. "Put your dick away, stranger," she said. "Let's cab it."

"Lucky bastard," she heard someone say. She gazed down at her new pet and couldn't agree more.

TESTING
THE WATER

Teresa Noelle Roberts

The conversation over dinner had been light, amusing, ordinary—first-date stuff but a promising first date. As long as they were in the restaurant, neither Serena nor Jack said a word about the subject that was on both their minds, the subject they'd been IM-ing about the past week, ever since Jack had made some joke about kinky sex and Serena had joked back, and then they'd had the ah-ha moment of realizing that the jokes weren't jokes at all, but a way of testing the water.

Turned out that Jack was more than a little bit kinky, and more than happy to learn his old friend had certain fantasies she'd love to explore.

But knowing that and actually making it happen were two different things.

They'd made it through dinner without saying a word about spanking, whips and chains, head games, any of the fascinating things they'd teased each other with so freely when they weren't face to face. Almost disappointingly ordinary, a typical "first date" between two people who'd been friends for awhile and had decided to take the plunge into something more, but weren't quite sure how to be romantic with each other.

Still, somehow, by the time they finished dessert, Serena had no question in her mind that she'd end up at Jack's place.

She was sitting on his leather couch like she'd done a hundred times before in the years they'd known each other. But this time the worn green leather seemed a lot more significant. And this time her pussy was pounding just from looking into his navy-blue eyes and imagining him actually doing some of the things they'd had the nerve to talk about from a safe distance.

Yet they were still talking about nothing. Or maybe about everything—classic cartoons, his work, favorite movies—but none of the things that mattered right at that moment.

Serena was trying desperately to come up with the proper segue. It was so much easier to talk about sex over the safety of IM than to look into a friend's eyes and admit you wanted him to spank you. Not to mention tie you up, and maybe put clothespins on your nipples, and all kinds of fascinating, scary stuff like that.

Luckily for her nerves, Jack got there first. "I still want to take you to the animation festival at the university. But let's talk about something more interesting now. How do you feel about erotic pain?"

Even though she was prepared for this turn in the conversation, even though she wanted it, she felt her face redden. Her eyes grew wide, and she said, a little breathily, "Please...I think. But we already talked about that..."

He smiled, and his smile was evil and delicious and everything she'd ever imagined it could be. "Over IM. In emails. But I wanted to see your face, to make sure you really want to feel my flogger or paddle or just my bare hand against your skin.

Because I know I'd love to redden your ass before I bent you over and fucked you, but I need to see in your eyes that you want that too."

The words touched Serena's core like skilled fingers. She squirmed, the leather couch tantalizing on her ass, but she couldn't form words to answer.

"That's a yes?"

She made herself speak. "Oh, God, yes." Then she took a deep breath, and tried to elaborate. "But I don't know what my limits are—I've never really done this before, just thought about it a lot—so I'm afraid I might... let you down." Suddenly, faced with the possible reality of all her longtime fantasies, she began to shake.

Jack, who had been standing in front of her looking hard and stern and glorious, sat down on the couch next to her and put his arm around her. "It's all right, Serena. You'll have a safeword. You *will* use the safeword if something is getting too much for you, either physically or emotionally, and I'll either tone it down or stop if that's what you need. And I won't be disappointed if you do."

Tension she hadn't been aware of fled her body, leaving her boneless but filled with another sort of tension, the good, anticipatory, nervous-but-excited kind. She leaned against Jack, and the heat of his skin through his summer clothes seemed to burn her. She wanted the clothes out of their way, wanted his hands on her, wanted him to pose her like a mannequin, strip her defenses away, spank her until she cried, fuck her senseless.

But he didn't. Instead, he seemed to wait for something.

She ventured a guess at what he was waiting to hear, based on her brief knowledge of him. "Calamari."

"What?"

"That'll be my safeword. In honor of what we had for dinner

tonight—and because it sure as hell isn't something I'd say by accident during sex."

He stood up and pulled her to her feet. "Now that that's settled, let's get on to the good stuff." There was laughter in his voice at her safeword, but when he said, "Undress," his tone changed. So did his posture, his bearing, the expression in those amazing blue eyes.

Serena had suspected he'd looked commanding before at times, a dominant in action. Now she realized she'd just gotten a taste of Jack. It wasn't that her old friend, the affable guy with the quirky sense of humor, disappeared. This man contained the one she'd first met, but he was more, in ways she couldn't quite describe yet.

All she knew was that she got her dress off in record time. The pretty little black lace bra she'd so carefully selected "just in case" disappeared under his stern gaze so quickly that she might as well have put on a white cotton basic. "Shoes?" she asked, the tremor in her voice surprising her.

"'Shoes, *Sir*,'" he corrected. "Leave them on for now."

She didn't know what she expected him to do first. But it certainly wasn't to stalk around her in a circle, looking at her body. She wasn't sure if she felt more like something on display at a museum or a prey animal being toyed with by some large predator, but whichever it was, it felt good. She awaited a command, a touch, anything, but for what seemed like an unaccountably long time, he just circled, studying her.

When he reached out, she expected a caress, or maybe a slap. Instead he put two fingers under her chin and raised her head a little. "Some doms may like a bowed head, but I don't. Look me in the eye when I speak to you. Your posture's decent, but you hunch your shoulders forward more than I like to see in a pretty woman. Too much time at a computer, I bet. So, clasp your hands behind your back—hold your own elbows, if you can."

She obeyed, aware of how it pulled her shoulders back and lifted her breasts.

"Better. Now open your legs a little. I don't want to see your legs closed unless I specifically say so."

She shifted, acutely aware of the slickness of her pussy. Moisture had gathered on the tops of her thighs. Was it visible? And would he like seeing how turned on she was, what a slut he made her feel like?

Yes, she decided, he probably would. You didn't get into this sort of thing if you liked shy, uptight girls. That was a curiously reassuring thought. She'd had a few relationships with guys—good guys she'd had a great time talking with before they'd started dating—who'd been intimidated by her sexuality even without knowing about all her kinks. Jack wouldn't be.

"Beautiful," Jack breathed. "Don't move. I'll be right back."

He vanished into another room, leaving her alone with her racing heart and her throbbing sex. The room seemed to tilt toward the direction he was heading, or maybe it was just all her attention following him.

He returned a few moments later with a collar of soft red leather. "When this is on, you will be mine: mine to command, mine to use as I see fit, mine to give pleasure or pain within the limits you've set and the protection of your safeword. When it's on, you call me Sir and I call you whatever I choose to call you"—here a bit of the humor she'd gotten fond of before she'd become interested in him as a potential lover flickered through the serious surface—"including late to dinner. And when it comes off, I'm Jack and you're Serena, and we're friends. Understood?"

She nodded, all the words she might want to say trapped in her throat.

And only when she nodded did he lift her hair, surprisingly gently, and fasten the collar around her throat.

The leather felt alive.

As soon as he fastened the buckle, she took a deep breath, then moved her head experimentally, reveling in the subtle pressure it exerted. Jack's hands slid from her throat to her shoulders, tracing trails of fire behind them.

"Do you like the collar?"

She still wasn't sure she could talk sensibly, but she managed, "Oh, yes, Sir. It feels wonderful. Natural." More than that, really. The leather felt like part of her, part of her skin or her soul that had been missing all along and had just been returned to her.

"Thought it might." His hands slid around to cup her breasts. Fingers clasped her nipples, gentle for an instant, then tightening, gripping. Fierce, hot, harder than anything another person had done to her nipples, as hard as she'd torment them when she was alone and craving something she'd never experienced from someone else's hands. Different, though, when Jack's hands did it—different and bone-meltingly good. "Harder," Serena begged. "Please, Sir. Harder."

"Greedy little slut," he breathed in her ear as he pinched down and twisted. "I like that in a woman."

Was it painful pleasure or pleasurable pain?

Did it matter?

All she knew was that her nipples had never been so happy before, or so directly connected to her dripping sex. Her knees wobbled. A desperate moan escaped her lips, and she worked her ass against him, feeling his hardness, wishing he'd get his pants out of the way so she could enjoy it properly.

And he didn't let up, not even when he bit down into the muscle of her shoulder.

More heat. More lust. "I could come from this," she managed to say, her voice broken and breathless.

He shook his head, teeth still clenched into her skin. Then he licked the tender spot and whispered, "Oh, no you won't. Not until I tell you to."

And that, paradoxically, was almost enough to push Serena over the edge.

One of Jack's hands snaked down her body to cup her sex—not stroking or caressing, exactly, but a gentle, possessive touch. Instinctively, she started to roll her hips, to push herself against him, but she took a deep breath, bit her lip, and just barely restrained herself from grinding down. "Good girl," he said. "Good, wet girl. I was going to toy with you a while longer and then take you into the bedroom, but instead I'm going to spank you here, right now. How do you like that idea?"

She hoped he hadn't wanted an articulate answer, because all she could do was groan something that she meant to be "Please" but was barely intelligible even to her own ears.

Jack guided her the few steps back to the couch, sat down, and patted his lap. "Over my knee, now!" Curt but not angry, just to the point. She couldn't have disobeyed if she'd wanted to. One hand pressed her face into the fragrant leather, and the other cracked down on her bare ass, right at the tender curve where bottom and thigh met, and she knew that this would be everything she'd hoped and possibly more.

"One good one on the sweet spot to get your attention." Jack's hand stroked gently over the now sensitive area, making the already wonderful ache even more delicious. "And then a bit of warm-up." A series of slaps, light but building in intensity, moving all over her cheeks but focusing on that area he called the sweet spot. So good. Stingy, but so good.

She rolled her hips, reaching up to meet his hand, then

pressing her mound into his leg, careful not to come but enjoying the sensations flowing through her. Broken whimpers poured from her throat.

Her whole ass felt warm and delightfully tender after a few minutes of this, and when he stopped and then moved the hand that was pressing her into the couch, she thought she might weep. She opened her mouth to protest, in fact, only to cry out as he slipped a hand under her and found her clit.

"Oh, yes," he said. "That's lovely. You do need this, don't you?"

Serena almost didn't recognize the voice that said, "Yes, Sir."

He worked his fingers skillfully, pushing her higher. The smell of her own juices and Jack's body, a little sweaty after the hot day, and the leather of the couch were blending, further teasing her senses. Her bottom was throbbing gently, deliciously, and his touch would have made her crazy even without the spanking beforehand. She felt herself starting to contract, tried to think of something distracting.

The idea of cleaning her kitchen held her off for a second.

Then he pinched a little and swirled his fingertips as if to soothe the pain he had just caused, and Serena wailed and bucked and ground her clit shamelessly against his hand as she came.

He bent down, kissed her shoulder. "Bad girl," he said. "I told you not to come until I gave permission." He sounded far more smug than displeased. "I guess I'm just going to have to spank you harder to teach you to behave. But since you've already come once, you might as well do it again if you can." He left his fingers on her clit. "Pleasure and pain. That's what it's all about."

And as his fingers kept caressing her, his other hand crashed onto her ass.

She flinched away instinctively, yelped with pain and surprise

—then gasped with delight. The heat and sting met the sensations from her clit somewhere deep inside her, creating a feeling like none she'd ever experienced, and she pushed her ass backward, eager for more.

Another hard smack, and another, and another, and all the while the fingers played on her clit. The pain spiraled, and so did the pleasure. Serena's world shrank to her body and Jack's hands.

"Come for me," Jack whispered. "Come now."

And she did, reaching her peak under a hard flurry of blows.

Jack stroked her back and ass gently as she trembled, and then drew her up and pulled her to sit in his lap, holding her almost as if she were a child as she clung to him.

Finally, the room stopped spinning. She opened her eyes, squirmed into a more comfortable position, and said, "Thank you, Sir."

"I'd ask how you liked it, but the orgasm gave it away. How does your butt feel?"

"Well, I can feel every fiber in your pants. I love it."

"And I can feel the heat through the fabric—which makes me want to feel your hot ass against me as I fuck you from behind. Would you like that?"

Seconds before, Serena had been blissfully boneless, and, she would have sworn, sated for the time being. The time being, it seemed, could be awfully short when Jack was around, because suddenly she wanted nothing more than Jack's cock inside her.

She wriggled off his lap. "Here?"

"Bedroom. I plan to wear you out, and you might as well have someplace comfortable to fall down."

She grinned.

They raced for the bedroom together.

NEVER
A ROOKIE

Craig J. Sorensen

P astrami on rye with fries, cheeseburger and fries, and a New York, rare, with a baker."

The familiar song of feminine voices was punctuated by syncopated snaps as tickets collected on the worn chrome order wheel.

"A Reuben with chips, and a club with fries."

"Ham and cheese omelette with home fries, two over easy with wheat toast and a short stack."

Sizzling of steaks and burgers, crackling of eggs on the grill, the hissing of flare-ups all blended with the rhythmic cycles of the dishwasher. The three servers practiced their dance in the narrow waitresses' station. Though it supported as many as eight waitresses at a time, there was always something special about the movements of a scant staff on these off-peak rushes.

Phillip noticed that this dance was different still on this day. The movements seemed more strained. A feather glide across the station by a seasoned waitress was interrupted by the clumsy steps of a rookie. Their hips collided and the veteran steadied her heavy tray.

"Goddamn it, girl!"

Phillip returned his focus to the order wheel, which still had two open spaces. He stepped up his pace to keep it that way. How he hated when orders started stacking along the silver counter.

Phillip recalled his first Saturday night in the restaurant, and his first job as a dishwasher. What seemed an eternity before had only been a year.

The dishes flowed in like high tide. Phillip had to struggle just to clean enough glasses, plates, and silverware to keep the restaurant from grinding to a halt. He hovered every moment on the verge of abject failure. Somehow, he got through, but that night, his favorite dreams of beautiful women ruthlessly ravishing his body were replaced by towers of dishes that loomed like midtown Manhattan.

Within just a few weeks he was the maestro. As he refined his skills, he found spaces to linger between flurries of activity. The raging hormones of a nineteen-year-old kicked in as he luxuriated between loads to graze on the smorgasbord of waitresses. Their uniforms were black one-piece dresses reaching no lower than mid-thigh. With the lace collars and hems, the uniforms conjured a French maid's outfit, especially with the small lace-trimmed white aprons where they pocketed their tickets, pens, tips, and after-dinner mints.

In only six months, Phillip had been promoted from the auspices of the sauna-like dishwasher to the oven-like front kitchen. Another first day, and he settled into the task of sandwich preparation while his new mentor worked the grill side. An early rush came in, and the wheel on Phillip's side of the kitchen

filled up. Orders began to stack on the counter while the waitresses continued an endless stream of demands. Like that first
day with the looming dishes, Phillip felt a welling desperation.
Flight instinct began to take hold.

His mentor, a fifteen-year veteran of the kitchen, started to
read the orders on Phillip's wheel. "I got it. I got it," Phillip
insisted.

"You sure? This is a pretty nasty rush. We don't want to
break you on your first day."

"I got it!" Phillip fumbled proudly through the mounting
orders. The mentor watched skeptically.

When the rush relented, Phillip had fought through it all by
himself. He felt an adrenaline rush like skiing down a slope of
densely packed snow peppered with moguls for the first time.
The order wheel hung askew like wind chimes in the calm after
a violent storm. The mentor gave him a thumbs-up.

Phillip looked out proudly at the waitresses. He felt the blood
rushing, focusing. He felt his zipper tighten. Perhaps it was just
beating the rush, or maybe the leggy, honey-haired, pre-law
student who picked up his last order had something to do with
it. She winked as she admired the club sandwich and corned beef
on rye—"looks delicious, babe!"

Pavlovian response or adrenaline, no matter. A nice, crisp
boner became the perfect closer in the cycle of the morbid rush
for Phillip, and so was his habitual short break in the walk-in
fridge, where he would sit on a box and cool down. A nice bottle
of Michelob fed his belly then soothed his groin until his desire
deflated.

Most of the staff didn't like to work Sundays. Except Phillip.
There was no hostess, no busboys, and the bar was closed. He
got to work both sides of the front kitchen, the grill and sand-

wich side. He even enjoyed running the dishwasher. A taste of his earliest glory days at the restaurant. Phillip loved to keep busy. There was nothing worse than being bored. But most of all, he loved Sundays because he was the only man on staff.

"Order up, Liz!"

Liz, a twenty-two-year veteran who was still nursing her anger at being pulled in on a Sunday, which she hadn't worked in over ten years, simply compressed her lips in a tight sneer. Her sinewy arm bulged as she balanced a late breakfast order deftly on her shoulder.

"Order up, Nancy! Is it Black fuckin' Friday and no one told us?"

Nancy, a brunette with a soft pleasant face and a curvy body, laughed. "It's Sunday, Phillip." She began to prepare her tray.

Phillip winked. "So it is. Order up, Wendy!"

Wendy was petite with a pretty heart-shaped face and large eyes. She was quiet and her cheeks sported a perpetual blush. This was her first Sunday, and this rush a rite of initiation. She had no frame of reference to answer Phillip's question, and she had no time for small talk. Her glance caught his only briefly as she arrayed the plates he had set on the counter onto her large tray, carefully balanced it on both hands, and teetered out to the floor.

There was no safety net on a Sunday. Minimal staff meant that rare rushes had to be handled with the precision of a commando raid. As the pressure rose, Wendy fell further behind. Liz, still angry that she was even there, began to browbeat the younger woman. "You got the smallest section in the place. Step it up! Two more of your tables need bussing and people are waiting. Get with it, girl!"

Phillip considered Liz's countenance. She was quite attractive. Her salt-and-pepper hair curved in close-cropped waves around her angular skull. The wrinkles that extended from her full lips and large eyes did more to amplify than diminish them.

Wendy's eyes began to dart with panic. Phillip had seen this happen more than once when a serious rush made some crumble like the Tacoma Narrows Bridge in that first unpredictable wind. "Get going! The elderly gentleman at table sixteen is about to leave. At least you should—"

As the humming dishwasher faded to rare numb silence, Phillip blurted, "Why don't you fuckin' help her, Liz? You're so goddamned good. Bus a couple of her tables, help her catch up! Were you never a rookie?"

Liz's jaw slowly dropped. Nancy froze then quickly fumbled through the silverware as if the loud clattering might diffuse the bomb that palpably ticked on top of Liz's shoulders. Wendy rushed out to the floor with a purposeful stride, leaving her loaded tray sitting on the counter.

Liz walked deliberately, like a gunfighter exiting the Long Branch Saloon, to face a snot-nosed, quick-handed wannabe rival. She entered the front kitchen, which waitresses never did, and stood toe to toe with Phillip. Phillip recalled in seventh grade when he stood up to the school bully, only to get the shit kicked out of him. This suddenly seemed a halcyon childhood memory. Liz's peppermint Life Saver breath issued from her slightly parted lips, but not a word came out. Radiant heat from her upper body eclipsed the grill.

Phillip's heart pounded like a death-metal bass drum pattern. He whispered, "Look Liz, the fact that you, one of our most experienced waitresses, and she, one of our least, are working on a Sunday should tell you something. They couldn't get anyone in here. What if she walks out? Nancy isn't the best waitress we ever had. You'd basically have to work the whole floor."

Liz bit her lip. The slightest curl of a smile cut to one side of her mouth, and her onyx eyes gleamed with the striped reflections of the overhead fluorescent tubes. She stepped even closer. Phillip did not back away. He did not breathe. She looked down at the front of his apron. He pulled his hips back trying to disguise the sudden bulge. Her eyes deepened. "I'll deal with you later."

Phillip turned around and twisted his cock like an hour hand from its awkward seven o'clock position to twelve o'clock high. He released the long-held breath and returned his focus to the relentless tide of orders.

In the shadow of the confrontation, Wendy burst into a flurry of activity. Fear, frustration, embarrassment, or a combination spurred the young woman like a lazy racehorse, startled by the whip to a defining realization that she didn't want to be at the back of the pack. In the midst of an impressive stream of activity, she paused as she picked up an order. Her gaze linked with Phillip's. Her eyes were backlit sapphires that circled large liquid ink pupils, alive and vibrant in a way Phillip had never seen from her. Her slim, translucent lips mouthed the words "Thank you."

The initial tension between Wendy and Liz began to morph. Despite the desperation as the rush continued, the waitresses became playful as they efficiently managed the floor. Liz stretched her body across Wendy's back as she helped the younger waitress find an odd size of glass in an upper cabinet. Wendy's hand rested on Liz's hip as she stepped around her to get a tray. Nancy squeezed to Wendy's side and reached across her to get silverware.

Phillip had always loved to watch the incidental contact as the waitresses navigated the slim station, but today was a command performance. As he set a plate on the counter, he stood on tiptoe and leaned forward while the three bent at the waist like synchronized swimmers. He took account of the lineup of buttocks: Wendy softly rounded and lean; Liz small, tight, and athletic; Nancy full and inviting.

He realized that a pair of upside-down eyes were on him. Liz had caught him admiring waitresses' bottoms, including hers, in the past. It had always seemed to touch a playful side, eliciting a wink. Not this time. Her teeth were clenched. It was obvious she hadn't forgiven him.

That mean look on her face made his cock feel heavy again. He turned quickly back to the grill, flipped a couple of steaks, and tried to ignore Liz's angry expression.

It was just after two when the rush finally receded. The waitresses began to restock their station. Bending hips exposed hidden reaches of shiny nylons. Breasts encased in tight dresses gave vistas to inviting warm valleys.

Never had Phillip needed his post-rush Michelob more.

He slipped into the walk-in and cracked a bottle; then took a mighty gulp. He put the bottle on his crotch like a cold compress. The door pronounced a soft wheeze, and Phillip shoved the half-empty bottle down to the side of the box and tried to act casual. Liz peered around the open door toward the waitresses' station, then looked back in at Phillip and let the door softly close. Phillip puzzled for a moment as he measured her menacing face, then tilted his head as he noticed Liz's legs were bare.

Her eyes locked on his. "Cooling down?"

"Yup."

She leaned to the side where the beer was stashed. He opened his leg to try to mask it. Liz's eyes narrowed to slits. She grabbed his knee and pushed it to the side to reveal the open Michelob. Phillip's eyes darted between her and the door.

"Drinking a beer on the job, and on a Sunday? You've been especially bad. And you should never have talked to me that."

"But Wendy really stepped it—"

"Quiet!"

Phillip drew a long breath. He opened his mouth to apologize, but the strange gleam in her eye made him hesitate. In the dim, cold light of the walk-in, her hard attractiveness, drenched in anger, grew staggering. As she planted her nude legs apart, his hardness began to throb. He rested his hands in front of his crotch.

She gripped his chin in her talon hand. "No two ways about it, you need to be punished."

Phillip's heart fluttered. He gulped a breath. Liz watched his face closely. Her hand began to release.

"Uh, yes—mistress?"

She nodded and stiffly slapped his cheek. "Stand up."

Phillip complied. She sat on the box and took his Michelob. She took a long drink while she untied his apron with the other hand. The apron fell to the cold floor. She stroked the large bulge at the front of his jeans. Phillip's hands instinctively moved toward his crotch.

"Hands on your head!"

He felt that familiar flight instinct. First big load of dishes, first overloaded order wheel, first time in the front kitchen alone. He looked at the door, then at Liz's demanding expression. She pulled his belt and pinched his knees between her bare thighs. Her strong hand settled on the front of his pants. He laced his fingers atop his head as she groped him, squeezing his hard cock firmly.

"Unhitch your pants."

Phillip hesitated, and she swatted his butt hard. "Now!" He unbuckled his belt. He paused and she swatted him again. The pain was startling. He unbuttoned his pants and they fell to his ankles.

"Step out." Another pause. A sharp, snapping slap on his chilling, bare butt. He stepped from his jeans and shoes. She tugged the bottom of his shirt. He obediently took it off, continually looking toward the walk-in door. She snapped his butt again. "Stop looking at that goddamned door! Bend over my knee!"

Phillip felt his mouth go slack and his eyes widen.

"Now, goddamn it!"

He leaned over and his hard rod slid between her dark thighs. Liz waited for a torturous moment. She smoothed his butt sensually. When he relaxed slightly, she snapped one cheek. He let out a yelp as she continued, spanking from cheek to cheek. "Don't you fucking ever, EVER—"

The walk-in door wheezed. Wendy stood at the slightly opened door.

"I told you to watch the goddamned floor!" Liz's eyes were wild.

"I— I—" Wendy started to back away.

"Wait, get in here."

Wendy stepped inside gingerly and let the door close. She folded her arms tight beneath her full breasts, then pushed her hands into her apron. She hesitated and then stretched her arms down her hips, back to beneath her breasts, all the while trying not to acknowledge the spectacle of Phillip's nude body over Liz's lap. Her eyes finally settled on him a few times, widening and lingering on each forbidden glance. A smile began to appear, though she seemed to be fighting it. She rolled her hips to one side.

"Take off your pantyhose and panties. Punishment without reward is pointless," Liz said to Wendy.

Tentatively, Wendy stepped from her pumps and reached up her short skirt. She peeled down her black nylons and bright red panties. An open-mouthed smile crossed her face. "Now lie on the floor," Liz commanded Phillip.

Phillip followed orders like a soldier taking a hill. The cold floor felt exquisite on his smoldering butt. Liz straddled his hips and motioned toward his face as if offering a seat on a bus. Wendy's shook her head in a soft "no," but it lacked conviction.

"Time for *us* to be rewarded."

"Oh please, please yes," Phillip whispered.

Liz took his cock in her hand and slid it under her dress. She squeezed him as she slowly drew down. Wendy took one last look at the door and slowly approached. Her stretching Cheshire smile was the last thing Phillip saw as her pussy eclipsed her face. She crushed tight to him. He kissed her folds, curled his tongue around her clit, and then traced her slim lips. Her soft moans of approval urged him to push his tongue as deep as he could, and she gave a yelp. Her juices flowed down his face.

Liz milked Phillip's stiffness. The two women's hands roamed his upper body. Ascending moans preceded the soft, wet pop of the women's deepening kisses. Phillip's hands took in the texture of their uniforms and then stroked their bare legs. His hand bumped Wendy's at the base of Liz's breast, and he caressed both. His other hand slid up Wendy's dress and beneath Liz's palm, which squeezed Wendy's hip. The six hands circled like bumper cars in triangular ravishes.

The women's knees squeezed Phillip breathless. The sound of their moans grew as first Liz's then Wendy's orgasms released, and stole his last tiny ounce of restraint. He lifted Liz's slim body high in the air, then continued to shudder into Liz until she collapsed to his drained, splayed body.

Wendy's hips pounded violently before she draped across Liz's hard back.

The three lay like stacked bodies smoldering on a winter battlefield. Finally Liz blurted. "Oh shit, we better get back out to the floor!"

"Where you been?" Nancy rushed toward the order wheel. She had seated five tables and was taking the orders as quickly as she could.

"Relax, we were just ironing out some differences." Liz smiled and patted Nancy's shoulder. "We'll get caught up in no time." Nancy's brow lowered as her eyes zeroed in on Liz's bare legs, then Wendy's.

Phillip seemed as cool as the walk-in as he tied a fresh apron around his hips and started all five orders in rapid succession. He tossed steaks and burgers on the grill, began some toast, and assembled a Reuben. "It's been one hell of a day, hasn't it, Nancy?"

Nancy's face was still crushed in anger as she measured his expression.

Though this wasn't really a rush, Phil felt that familiar stirring.

Liz grinned at Nancy and rested her hand on Nancy's while she stepped around to fill some glasses of ice water. "We'll be caught up in no time, Nancy, and it's only a couple hours 'til closing."

Phillip nodded. "Yeah, and this is all my fault, Nancy. You can deal with me however you see fit after closing."

Nancy's brow rose like a drawbridge. She looked at Wendy and then Liz.

Liz shrugged. "We'll help if you like."

Wendy's cheeks glowed like emergency lights at a four-alarm fire. She nodded then lowered her head.

Nancy's mouth curled slowly into a gleaming smile.

Liz peered over the counter as a thick ridge grew on the front of Phillip's apron. "Such a bad boy, but not beyond redemp-tion."

PROVOCATION

Jay Lawrence

I hate this place."

My voice sounded shrill but I didn't care.

Art raised an eyebrow. "Give it a chance. We've only seen the airport and the suburbs of Phoenix. It'll improve."

I crossed my legs and pouted. The A/C was turned up high, blasting cold air on my chest. My nipples were hard. Ahead, the poker-straight highway stretched into the shimmering distance. I was tired, hungry, thirsty, and horny but didn't have the sense to voice any of those needs in an adult fashion.

"I wish we'd stayed in New Jersey."

"Any more of this, sweetheart, and *I'll* wish you'd stayed at home, too."

Here was the cue I'd been waiting for and I pounced, eager for a fight, my libido so misplaced it wasn't funny.

"I *should* have fucking stayed at home! Christ, I'm so hot..."

"So I see."

The edge of amusement in Art's maddeningly calm voice made me want to slap him. I hated his self-control, longed to scratch my nails down his back and draw blood. Yep, I was horny...

"Why are you pulling over?"

The car drew into a rest area, and Art got out without a word. I watched him head into the men's washroom without a backward glance. I uncrossed my legs, the moist flesh of my thighs sticking together beneath my shorts.

Christ, just fuck me. Fuck me hard and bite my neck and stick your finger in my ass. Give it to me hard, will you?

I didn't realize, back then, that my penchant for rough sex was a hint about some darker needs. I only knew I liked to be pinned down, legs thrust over my head, and fucked so deep and strong I thought his cock would come out of my mouth.

I thought about sex, and my nipples hardened even more. I wasn't wearing a bra, and they pushed against the thin cotton of my T-shirt.

"Drink this."

Art returned with a paper cup full of water.

"I'm not thirsty."

I watched him drink the cup in one big swallow. A few drops ran down his chin and swiftly evaporated.

"Fuck you," I muttered, my mouth dry, panties wet.

"I don't fuck silly girls."

Wild with hormones, I pinched his thigh through his jeans, as hard as I could. Strange foreplay but it worked for me.

"Do that again and I'm going to whip your ass, Joely."

I paused. It was that look-into-the-abyss-and-decide-whether-to-jump moment. I could have pulled back. I didn't.

Slyly, I reached out and slowly, deliberately, pinched him on the other thigh. Not a smart thing to do to an ex-Marine.

Art threw open the car door. I watched his tall, spare frame cross the baking tarmac of the rest area and disappear behind a line of eucalyptus trees. Damn him. I didn't know whether to stay and sulk or go see what he was up to.

I'm going to whip your ass, Joely.

Art's words were like a searing brand on my overheated brain. Whip my ass. Something about the idea excited me. I felt angry and nervy but incredibly turned on. A lone trucker watched me as I climbed out of the car and walked slowly across the rest area. I knew the guy was admiring my ass, tight and round in skimpy white shorts. I thought about fucking him, screwing a nameless stranger just for the hell of it. Where was Art?

Intense heat beat down on my bare head. Suddenly, I felt like a little girl, left alone and looking for Daddy.

"What kept you?"

There was a picnic area behind the row of dusty trees, with a long table and bench seats. Art leaned against the table. I realized, with a shock that made my heart jump, that he had taken his belt off and held it, looped, in one hand. "Bend over the table and pull down your shorts."

I stared at him. Was it a joke? His brown eyes gazed levelly back at me without a hint of humor. Shit.

"But we can't. Not *here*..."

My voice trailed away to nothing and butterflies danced in my stomach. I thought of my naked ass, shorts around my ankles, Art's heavy black belt cracking down on my unprotected cheeks. Slowly, dragging my feet, I approached the picnic table.

"Drop 'em."

My fingers trembled as I undid the button and pulled down the zip. In a few moments the tight shorts were a crumpled heap about my ankles, swiftly followed by my panties.

"Bend right over. Your body flat against the table."

It felt like a dream. I thought about the truck driver and wondered if he was watching, imagined him jerking off as Art whipped my ass.

"You really need this."

I spread my thighs and felt a drop of pussy juice dribble down my sweat-sticky flesh. My cunt was slick. I wanted to be whipped and whipped hard. My breasts were crushed beneath me as I assumed the position. I felt the cool surface of the leather belt against my asscheeks.

Art placed his free hand on the small of my back, and I shivered uncontrollably.

"You going to talk to me like that again?"

I shook my head.

"What did you say, Joely?"

I swallowed hard. My voice was raw with sex.

"No, Art."

Cool leather left my skin, and there was a taut pause and then a loud crack. I jumped as if I'd been shot and cried out in shock. It damn well hurt.

"I should've done this months ago."

I wanted to reach back and rub my smarting bottom. Instead, I gripped the warm edge of the picnic table and thrust my ass higher, pushed it toward Art, inviting another taste of the belt. I still don't know why. It hurt like hell, but it was a good kind of pain, one I needed to feel.

I cried out as a second sharp, hot lash cut across my trembling, vulnerable bottom. That time I jumped, my whole body convulsing in reaction to the belt. Heat was all around—beating down on my body from the cloudless desert sky and warming up my naked squirming ass. My top clung to my back as I began to sweat. My pussy was wet. Where the hell was that truck driver? Random, lust-filled thoughts passed through my mind as Art began to whip me in a steady rhythm.

The leather stung like biting insects. I jumped and jolted and wriggled and squirmed about, dancing from one foot to the other, jiggling around but always offering my ass to the belt again and again. I hated the pain, but I wanted it too. The blows hurt and yet made me feel more aroused than I'd ever felt in my life. Where *was* that truck driver? I realized that I wanted him to watch me getting my bare bottom whipped. I wanted to lie over a table in the open air with my shorts round my ankles and my boyfriend taking his belt to me. I wanted the stranger to get off on my humiliation, take his cock out, and jerk off all over my face.

The whipping ended, and I felt a sense of something missing, disappointment, though I'm not sure I could have taken much more. I realized my face was very hot, as warm as my well-lashed ass. Art's hand caressed my bottom and I shuddered, ready to come.

His fingers slid down to my pussy and I groaned. I needed release. I thrust my hips at Art, fucking his searching hand.

"I don't think I've ever seen you so wet and ready."

It was true. Something about being whipped had really turned my crank.

"Now you're going to go stand over by that tree with your shorts round your ankles. It's corner time, Joely."

"What?"

My eyes must have been as wide as Bambi's. Now, my darling boyfriend wanted me to parade myself, half naked, where anyone could pass by and see my well-whipped ass. We'd both be arrested.

"I can't do that..."

Without a word, Art pulled me up and marched me toward the nearest tree. I shuffled along with my shorts restricting my movement like a convict's manacles. The shade felt refreshingly cool. I could see the nearby rest area. There were a few vehicles parked on the tarmac. Anyone could decide to take a walk over to the picnic table. I felt oddly powerless, a little desperate. Once more, this was a new sensation, and something about it turned me on.

"You'll do as you're told, Joely. Face the tree. No, don't try to cover your ass with your hands. I'm going to sit here and admire my handiwork. That's a well-whipped behind you've got there."

The bark felt rough beneath my chest and thighs. I did as I was told like a good little girl, the sense of arousal growing steadily in my cunt and mind. I started thinking about going over Art's knees for a long, hard, bare-bottom spanking. I thought about paddlings and whippings and being severely chastised with a riding crop. Visions of discipline danced in my head.

"You look good, sweetheart."

I didn't know how to respond. To thank Art for the compliment seemed strange under the circumstances. I felt excited, exposed, nervy. Any moment, someone could approach and witness my al fresco corner time. My heart thumped, and my legs shook a little. My ass felt very warm, throbbing in time to the tingling of my clit. I needed release.

Minutes passed. I could hear insects and traffic passing on the highway. I didn't want to move. I wanted to do as I was told. Obeying Art aroused me.

"Come here, Joely."

I turned and looked at Art. He was sitting on the bench by the picnic table, and he patted his lap. I shuffled toward him, feeling a strange mix of embarrassment and excitement. I could see his cock pressing hard against the fly of his jeans. He wanted me to suck him off. I began to crouch down between his legs, but he stopped me.

"Just to make sure the message is clear."

Art grabbed me and put me across his knees. With a sharp intake of breath, he began to spank me, hard and fast on my sore bottom. I squealed.

"You're going to learn to do as you are told, young lady!"

My hips writhed and bucked over his thighs. I made rapid fucking movements, grinding myself against his legs. I was going to come.

Art's hand felt very different from his belt, almost more arousing, intimate. I felt like a naughty little girl. I could feel my warm ass becoming hotter. I was going to have trouble sitting down.

Art spanked me good and hard, my naked bottom quivering with every short, sharp slap. My clit was swollen fit to burst. My pussy dripped juice on my boyfriend's thighs. I was going to come.

"Oh please!"

I orgasmed violently, kicking my legs and crying out in pleasure and pain. Confused and trembling, I lay there, my shorts still wrapped about my ankles.

"Now, you're going to go to the women's washroom, make yourself tidy, and have a big drink of water."

I nodded, unable to speak. Slowly, I stood up and wriggled into my shorts. The fabric felt cool against my hot, well-whipped and spanked behind.

"Run along. We haven't got all day."

"Yes, Art."

I could barely place one foot in front of the other as I walked to the washroom. When I came out, after drinking several cups of much needed water, I saw the truck driver. He was leaning against a mailbox looking at me in a way that made me feel strange inside. A kind of predatory smile, amused, hungry. He knew. He had watched my spanking. I walked quickly away, ignoring him, feeling his eyes burn into my back, knowing he was watching my wriggling ass, remembering it taking Art's belt. I ran back to the car. Art smiled at me in a way I hadn't seen him smile before.

"Things are going to be a bit different from now on, sweetheart."

My ass tingled and burned as I sat down.

"Yes," I agreed, and with a little jolt, I realized that I didn't miss New Jersey at all.

I PROMISE TO DO MY BEST

Teresa Joseph

The twenty-three-year-old woman might never have been a real member of the Guide's Association, but standing there in her smart, old-fashioned uniform as she gave the Guide's salute, she literally trembled with anticipation as the troop leader sat down and crossed her long, smooth legs.

Since the day her first girlfriend had pulled her across her knee and smacked her naked bottom, Natalie Burrows had been so obsessed with corporal punishment that she'd barely been able to think straight.

From dressing up as a sexy little schoolgirl to paying Mistress Raven £100 an hour to punish her firm young cheeks, the gorgeous blonde had done everything in her power to satisfy her fetish. And so when one of the doms at a BDSM fetish nightclub told Natalie about a lesbian CP society that parodied the Girl Guides, the desperate woman became so excited that she joined the next day.

After three years of playing the stern headmistress for sexy young lesbians like Natalie, Michelle Redding had struck upon the idea of forming a lesbian Guide Troop three years earlier whilst driving though the New Forest.

"Sitting around the campfire, toasting marshmallows and singing Kumbaya…" She'd sighed dreamily. "Getting the girls to make switches and paddles out of the surrounding trees and branches, then beating each of their gorgeous bottoms until they're all toasted as well."

And a few days later, having bought all the uniforms and equipment she would need on eBay, the Guider had initiated her first twelve members, and the spanking had begun.

No matter how many women might have joined the troop over the last few years, however, Michele was always more than willing to accept a new member. And as Natalie changed into her new uniform and recited the Guide's pledge, the troop leader grinned with anticipation as she waited to punish her rump.

"I promise to do my best, to serve the Queen, and do my duty to God," recited the dutiful initiate, desperate to feel the woman's hand against her rump. And then hitching the skirt of her uniform up around her waist, Natalie slipped her knickers down as she lay across her lap.

"Are you ready to earn your first merit badge?" teased the Guider as she lovingly caressed Natalie's naked bottom.

"Yes, Madam," whimpered Natalie as she began licking her lips. And as the Guider gently warmed her buttocks with the flat of her hand, her whole body began to tingle with desire as the pussy juice poured from her slit.

After a few gentle taps across the bottom to help set the mood, however, Natalie panted with lust as the real punishment began.

It was absolutely relentless.

With a smooth, even rhythm that would put a metronome to

shame, the Guider firmly smacked each new member's cheeks in turn. And although it didn't seem to hurt at first, as the smacks began to multiply, turning her warm, blushing bottom a gorgeous shade of pink, Natalie winced and whimpered with discomfort.

"Do you still want to join my troop?" asked the Guider as she shifted into second gear, doubling the speed and ferocity of Natalie's punishment whilst savoring her gasps of pain.

"Yes, Madam!" cried Natalie, struggling to resist the urge to cover her flaming rump. "I want to be a Guide! I want to be a good girl and do my duty to...*God!*"

But no matter how much she might have longed to let the Guider spank her rump, it wasn't long before self-preservation forced her to cover herself, and the Guider had to pin her arms up behind her back.

She panted desperately. *"Oh God! Please! Jesus Christ!"*

But the Guider wasn't deterred.

"Are you praying, darling?" she laughed mischievously, never stopping or slowing down for a single moment as the bright red handprints began to form across the new girl's rump. And as she shifted Natalie's punishment into third gear, the poor girl started howling uncontrollably as the pain spread across her naked cheeks.

Right on schedule, the sexy blonde initiate started kicking and struggling as the tears streamed down her face. But no matter how much she might have screamed or pleaded, Natalie's pussy was still tingling with pleasure, and she never really wanted it to stop.

After ten long minutes of agonizing punishment, every inch of Natalie's bottom was a deep, blazing crimson, and her beautiful face had turned the same color as the tears streamed down her cheeks. But as the Guider picked up her round leather paddle and put it to good use, it wasn't long before the initiate's bottom was as purple as could be.

The helpless woman begged for mercy as Miss Redding furiously paddled each of her buttocks in turn, the smooth round leather becoming red-hot as it smacked her naked cheeks.

Her bottom was so sore and swollen that she felt like she might never be able to sit down again. And by the time the Guider had picked up the twin-tongued leather tawse, Natalie could hardly remember what her bottom had felt like before her initiation had begun.

Dozens of dark welts formed across the new girl's buttocks as the razor-sharp leather sliced into her swollen cheeks; forcing Natalie to bite her lip until she practically drew blood. And although she sighed with relief as the Guider began smacking the back of her thighs with the flat of her hand again, her bottom was still on fire, and it wouldn't be long before the backs of her thighs would begin burning as well.

It took less than two minutes for the Guider to turn the woman's thighs the same gorgeous shade of pink. And squealing with agony as long, slender twigs of the sharp birch began cutting into her skin, Natalie could already tell that the blazing red welts would be with her for many weeks to come.

"Stand and salute!" commanded the Guider, finally releasing Natalie's wrists from her vice-like grip. And the moment she was free, Natalie leapt onto her feet.

At this point, most of Michelle's initiates would have run screaming out the front door, never to be seen again. But biting her lip to help endure the pain as she stood at attention, holding up three of the fingers of her right hand whilst holding her left hand behind her back, Natalie barely batted an eyelid as she waited for the second phase of her punishment to begin.

"Recite the Guide's Pledge," ordered Miss Redding as she started smacking the front of Natalie's thighs, using the same smooth, even rhythm that had set her cheeks ablaze.

Natalie obeyed without a moment's hesitation.

"I *promise...to do my...BEST!*" She yelped and whimpered as her burning thighs turned the same blushing shade of pink. "To serve the...*Oh God! Please Stop!*"

But the Guider never missed a single stroke.

"Silly girl!" she snapped derisively, smacking each thigh twice as hard to emphasize the point. "Now you'll have to start all over again!"

And although Natalie longed to obey her new Guider, the pain was too much to bear.

"I promise to...*Oh fuck!*"

"Start again!"

"I promise to...*Jesus Christ!*"

"And again!"

It took more than a dozen attempts for Natalie to recite the entire pledge without a single plea for mercy as she gasped for air and pulled away from the Guider's furious stroke. And by the time she was finished, Natalie's thighs were burning like a campfire and covered with blazing red handprints.

Needless to say, the experienced Guider was more than impressed with Natalie's phenomenal endurance. This sexy little blonde had proven beyond a doubt that she wanted to be a member of her troop and that she'd be able to take whatever was dished out. But before she could receive her first merit badge, however, Natalie had one last hurdle to clear.

"You will *walk* the entire length of the course with your fingers laced above your head," instructed the Guider, as the rest of the troop took a studded leather paddle and prepared to beat her buttocks black and blue. "If you run, skip, jump, or take your hands away from your head, you will have to start all over again. And when you finish the course, you will have earned your 'Endurance' badge. Clear?"

Natalie nodded obediently. But as the first set of cold metal studs bit deep into her swollen buttocks, the pain was so unbearable that she didn't think that she'd ever be able to finish.

Placing one foot in front of the other as slowly as she could, Natalie clenched her fingers together until her knuckles turned white as each Guide beat her naked buttocks in turn. And when she'd finally finished the course, the new Guide sat down on the pile of ice cubes that Miss Redding had provided, wailing uncontrollably but still feeling as happy as could be as the Guider presented her with her first merit badge.

"And in two months, you'll be able to try for your second merit badge," laughed one of the other Guides as they all gathered round to congratulate the new member.

But Natalie wasn't sure if her buttocks would have healed by then, and so she decided to play it safe.

"Better make it three," she murmured happily.

Three months later, when the swelling had gone down, the blue-and-purple welts had healed, and the memory of the pain had faded, Natalie returned to the Guide's headquarters for another night of blazing crimson ecstasy.

"Remember, girls," instructed the Guider as she marched back and forth across the room, "Try to cane each other's buttocks as hard as you possibly can."

Natalie paired off with an experienced guide named Rebecca, a sweet little redhead who loved corporal punishment and had the merit badges to prove it. And having whacked the long, painful bamboo rod across Rebecca's gorgeous cheeks, Natalie gritted her teeth with anticipation as she bent right over, touched her toes, and prepared to receive another vicious stroke across her rump.

Every Guide in the room was screaming as the huge, stinging welts swelled across their naked rumps. But still rubbing her naked bottom with one hand as she prepared to cane her partner, she drew the bamboo cane far back behind her head and laid it full square across Natalie's swollen buttocks; forcing the sexy blonde to squeal in pain before passing the cane back to her and bending down to receive another stroke herself.

Without allowing the girls to wipe their tears away or to soothe their throbbing cheeks, once the punishment was over, the Guider ordered the girls to stand side by side with their hands behind their heads as she inspected each bottom in turn. And if one of the girls' welts wasn't as swollen as it could have been or if the line was crooked, she ordered the Guide to bend over while she corrected the problem.

With the speed and accuracy of Zorro cutting a Z into someone's clothing, Miss Redding could lay up to a dozen cutting strokes across a woman's rump before she even had a chance to notice the pain. And having decided to lay a beautiful crisscross pattern across Josephine's rump, Miss Redding allowed the girl to jump around the room as she set to work on the next girl's bottom.

In the name of fairness, with sadistic delight, Miss Redding proceeded to lay a crisscross pattern across each of the other Guides' bottoms in turn, ordering them to bend over and making them yowl in pain as the swollen welts began to throb across their cheeks.

By the time she had finished, it looked as if the Guides were taking part in a sack race whilst the sacks were on fire; furiously rubbing their naked buttocks as the tears poured down their cheeks. And having invested in a two-liter tube of ice-cold moisturizing cream, the Guider allowed each of them to smear some across their naked cheeks. It wasn't long before the tub was completely empty.

As she struggled in vain to soothe the flaming sting across her bottom, Natalie was beginning to understand why this Guide troop only held meetings once a month. But as the Guider instructed them all to get back into pairs and to "help rub each other better," she began to wish she could go there every day.

Passionately kissing each other's tear-stained lips as they rubbed the soothing moisturizer into each other's bottoms, Natalie and Rebecca could not decide if they were in agony or lust.

A couple of the sobbing women even decided to "help rub each other better" by greedily licking each other's dripping pussies as the tears flowed. And as they eagerly kissed and caressed each other's naked bodies, it wasn't long before all of the other Guides had followed suit.

"Isn't anyone going to lick my pussy?" demanded the Guider as she watched her whole troop descend into wailing Sapphic delight.

"I will, Madam," sobbed Natalie as Rebecca eagerly lapped the last of the pussy juice from her swollen clit.

And as Natalie knelt between Miss Redding's gorgeous thighs, it wasn't long before the new Guide had earned her second merit badge.

Before she sent her Guides home, however, Miss Redding reminded each of them that they needed to have designed and built a functioning CP implement before next month's meeting; something that any member of the troop could make out of ordinary camping equipment and twigs or branches.

"Imagine that you've gone on a camping trip and your girlfriend's forgotten to secure the tent," she explained as the girls changed back into their normal clothes and got ready to leave. "Design me something that you can put together in two minutes and that will leave her wincing for days."

And although it took quite awhile for Natalie to come up

with a suitable idea, it didn't take her long to design something that made her wince with desire.

"Very nice," praised the Guider at next month's meeting, lashing the makeshift cat-o'-nine-tails back and forth to test its whipping action. "Very nice indeed."

Natalie brought two pairs of leather hiking straps and a roll of waterproof duct tape to the meeting that evening. In less than thirty seconds, she had knotted the straps together and secured the handle with a length of tape, creating a truly vicious-looking CP implement that she longed to feel against her cheeks. And so when the Guider decided to put it to the ultimate test, Natalie eagerly pulled her knickers down.

"How does it feel?" teased the Guider as the first stroke sliced into Natalie's naked buttocks, leaving half a dozen razor-thin, flaming red welts that would sting for days to come. "Does it feel lovely?"

But gripping her beautiful ankles as hard as she could, Natalie was too busy trying not to scream to be able to reply.

In fact, as the seventh stroke hit her swollen cheeks, the urge to run was almost impossible to resist. But closing her eyes and gritting her teeth, Natalie managed to keep her composure by reciting the first line of the Guide's Pledge over and over again.

"I promise to do my best!" She wept pathetically. "I *promise* to do my best!"

The Guider was so impressed with Natalie's endurance that she decided to test the other Guides' CP implements across her naked cheeks as well.

"*I PROMISE TO DO MY BEST!*" Natalie shrieked uncontrollably as the homemade birch rod cut deep into her tender, naked thighs. "*I PROMISE TO DO MY BEST!*"

PARTY MANNERS

Morgan Aine

My collar threatened to choke me. Each breath was a labor.

I had been dreading this function for weeks. But the party John was holding, for this group of friends, meant a lot to him. The hotel suite had been prepared earlier by the caterers. This was the second social event that had come up since we began seeing each other, and the first had been brutal. The memory of his friends' reactions left its mark. They thought me second-rate and trite. I wouldn't say out loud what I thought of them.

Our entrance to the suite was duly noted. The silence that ensued spoke volumes. Heads turned and mouths hung open. Here was the entrance he expected and the one I dreaded. Everyone in the room took note. My skimpy dress barely covered the tops of my stockings. There was no place for me to hide.

John's failed marriage was a hot gossip topic. No one could understand why he'd left his wife. The couple appeared to have it all. Everyone wanted to be them. Very few people knew his wife privately. Her lack of self-control had been her ruin. She'd had problems keeping her legs together around the hired help. John caught her time and time again. Her lack of loyalty annoyed and infuriated him. It pushed them apart and ultimately ended their marriage.

What made me especially desirable to him was that I was the perfect submissive. Nothing could pry me away. From the moment we'd gotten together, his dominance over me was complete. My level of admiration and trust in him was enormous. His faith in me was the same. I neither needed nor wanted anyone else. He filled me up.

Now, John casually carried my leash between his fingers. He fondled the handle lovingly, his grip light and loose. Every person in the room seemed to have their eyebrows raised. The heat of their gazes washed over me. My skin darkened blood red from my face down across my breasts. I swallowed deeply and tried to keep from panicking.

I had begged him to reconsider this public display of our personal relationship. The vanilla-ness of these people had almost drowned me the last time. I wasn't sure I could handle another attack. Almost all of the couples knew his ex-wife. They didn't give a damn if they embarrassed me or hurt my feelings. I was nothing to them.

Yet John felt it important to be himself. He didn't care what people thought of his little eccentricities. He relished the thought of keeping people off balance. His openness in exposing his dominant personality had been a long time in the making. His ex-wife's infidelities had taught him that social priority didn't matter. Whoever you are in your core is who you are. No sense in trying to hide from the world.

It took a lot less time for the conversation to resume than I had imagined. After their initial shock, the guests dealt with the situation by ignoring us.

We made our way through the crowded room, John pausing here and there to speak with his friends. I followed around behind him as he greeted a few close associates. I smiled quietly at everyone, and although I noticed the rude glances, I didn't let them register very deeply. As a submissive, I knew my place.

John and I worked our way to the bar. I leaned my back against the padded edge.

John ordered. Gin for me, whiskey for him. Within moments, I had my drink in hand. I gripped the icy glass in my palm and tried to relax. John's eyes kept questioning me. But I knew better than to try to answer an unspoken question.

A group of men were standing by the window talking. There was only one I recognized. Peter had been at the last party I attended. His wife had a way of bringing out the worst in me. I was thankful I had avoided her so far.

I saw rather than heard one of them motion to John. He hesitated briefly before responding.

"Behave," John advised.

Dropping the handle of the leash to my hand, he patted it before walking away. I gulped my gin and tonic. Nerves played me. I hoped he wouldn't be gone long. It was hard to stand alone.

I eavesdropped on the couple next to me. Their conversation centered on my collar and leash. I strained to hear them as a way of occupying my time. I could see a guy working his way over to me from the corner of my eye. It took a full five minutes for him to approach. Half turning, I set my drink down and busied myself, tapping the leash handle against my upturned palm. I avoided eye contact, but he was insistent that he get my attention. His voice was loud and invasive.

"So you're his slut, eh?"

My back stiffened.

"Cat got your tongue?" He was clearly drunk. His voice carried. I knew if I didn't respond he would only get louder.

"You'd have to ask John that. He normally calls me his whore." My insolence dripped like syrup. I hoped if I mocked him, he would stop.

My impertinence was marked by his stare. But I refused to back down.

"Does that mean anyone can fuck you?"

I considered my options, then I looked across the room at John. He was deeply engrossed in conversation. I couldn't expect him to rescue me. I was in this alone.

"I said," I tried to keep my voice level, "you would have to ask John. It's his decision." Even as I spoke these words, I knew the answer. John wouldn't share me with anyone. It was part of our original agreement. I said it because I wanted to get a rise out of this asshole.

"Really," I continued to goad him, "you should ask him. You never know. He might just let you."

For emphasis, I dragged my fingers through the neckline of my dress revealing most of my left breast. The edge of my nipple poked out of my bra. I slid my other hand down my side and gathered the hem into my grip. Tugging slightly, I exposed the skin above my stocking. The move accented the muscle along my thigh.

With precision, I ran my tongue over my lips and smiled seductively. His hand snaked out and landed directly on my breast. Instinct ruled. I slapped him. It was a natural reaction, and I did it without thinking.

Almost instantly, I felt John's hand grip my upper arm. His voice was loud, blasting in my ear.

"Do you need something, Don?" He asked. "Is Jordan being difficult?"

John's eyes cut into me, and I shook my head at him in disbelief. Surely he wasn't going to blame me for this?

"No...John...She...I..." Don stammered like a drunken fool. "I stumbled, fell against her. She thought I was coming on to her." He covered his tracks.

"He was talking trash." I was quick to explain. "Really, John. Listen. He wants to know if he can fuck me. I told him to ask you."

John laughed loudly. His grip tightened on my arm. He laughed again before answering.

"Well, if that's the question, Donald, the answer is 'fuck no,' but I can understand why you would want to. Jordan is a beauty. She sucks cock well, too, but I am keeping that for myself. I'm selfish that way. You'll just have to take my word for it. I'm sure you understand."

He jerked me toward him and took the leash handle from my hand. His other hand pushed my dress down farther. His fingers worked into my bra, exposing my breast. With confidence, he pinched the nipple and worked it between his thumb and forefinger. I gasped as he squeezed. My panties dampened. Don's eyes nearly popped out of their sockets.

The assault ended as abruptly as it started. John slapped Don on the back to help him get his tongue restored to his mouth.

"Excuse me while I take care of something, Don. Forgive me for not staying to chat."

With that said, John grabbed my leash close to the collar. He pulled me away from the bar and through an opening on the left. He kicked the door partially closed with the heel of his boot. My heart pounded.

We entered a bedroom that was doubling as a coatroom. The white bedspread was spattered with jackets and purses. I took this in, but it barely registered. John's swift movements kept me from protesting. He sat on the bed and pulled me across his knees.

Within seconds, he had my dress hiked up and my panties down. The coolness of the air hit me. Goosebumps ripened my skin. I sensed his hand as it cascaded down, barely having time to tighten my muscles before he made contact. The sting was instantaneous. The pop seemed loud in my ears. I gasped once before the next strike came. The moisture in my pussy drained to the outer lips. He always got this reaction. It was what he wanted.

He stroked his fingers over the palm print.

"I told you to behave." Once again, his palm found a spot. I was panting hard. I couldn't speak.

"You should have walked over to me."

Again, his hand met my skin.

"You didn't have to let it go that far."

Each statement was punctuated by a smack.

"You knew better."

I tried to face him, but he held me firm. I could see into the other room. There was a crowd of people gathering close enough to stare inside. They seemed shocked but continued to gawk. Not one of them turned away. His actions held them mesmerized. The expressions were priceless. The only thing I could do was close my eyes and bury my face against his thigh.

After several more slaps, I stopped fighting him. Best to let him get it over with. My thighs and cheeks were inflamed. The stinging sensation washed over me. I pushed my pussy against him. The climax was immediate. Throbbing replaced the ache. I panted to catch my breath.

He finished me off by rubbing his palms hard into my flesh, keeping the burn on the surface. I knew the sting would last for quite some time. He wanted me to have a reminder for the rest of the evening. Carefully he tangled his fingers in the hair on the back of my neck and pulled me upright. His mouth crashed onto mine as he sealed his ownership. "Now, can you behave, pet?"

I nodded, yes. Every ounce of my focus was on him. All others became insignificant.

"Answer me," he prodded.

"Yes."

My face was as bright as my ass, but I kept my eyes downcast. I loved that he owned me. This would leave no doubt in their minds.

"Good girl." He forced me to stand and rose up beside me. Grasping my leash, he tugged me back to the party. The onlookers parted to allow us through. I could feel the penetration of their gazes from behind me. I knew that the evidence of his spanking was viewable below the hem of my dress.

I wasn't sure which cheeks were the reddest, but it didn't matter.

I belonged to him.

TROPHY BUCKLE

Rakelle Valencia

What did you say to me?"

Jed looked down at his glass.

The one and only drinking establishment in town was empty. It was Tuesday night, and the regulars had blown their weekly wad since sundown on Sunday. The bar was dim with the warm, yellowish glow of the wagon wheel lamp that hung too low from the ceiling. Many had whacked their head on it when buzzed enough not to be careful or not to care. The polyurethaned pine walls reflected the sallow lighting off its polished surface. And the place was small with a heavy mahogany bar trimmed in brass hoarding at least a third of the space.

Beth gazed at him fiercely, daring him to repeat the come-on he'd just offered. He didn't want to, and yet one part of him did.

Jed sat on a worn, scratched stool continuing to drink. He couldn't look at Beth. The summer had been long, and the work sorting and shipping cattle at the end of the hot season made it longer knowing that beef prices were low, feed prices were high, and the few well-started colts he would be able to sell to city buyers could only get him supplies enough to survive the winter. But at least he could afford supplies. Many ranchers were turning their homesteads over to developers. They just couldn't make it.

Beth turned away to place the tall, clean glass on the rack above the long bar mirror. A clink of glass resounded in the empty room. She walked out from behind the bar to the door, flipped over the sign to read "closed," pulled the shade, and clicked the lock.

Jed downed the whiskey, feeling it sear his throat to the pit of his gut. He set the glass on the wooden bar and watched as Beth approached. She was as handsome as back in those high school days, ten or fifteen years ago now. Beth was never considered delicate or pretty. But she had sex appeal wrapped up in a strong, sturdy way that said "bring it on" without coming across as loose.

She took hold of his belt, popping the trophy buckle as she stared him directly in the eyes. Jed sat there, hands relaxed on his thighs, listening to the rasping his thick leather belt made as it was liberated from his Wranglers.

A quick flick of her wrists looped the leather over his brown felt Stetson and smacked it against the back of his neck. With the tails in her hand, she dragged him off the stool and under a dangerously low-hanging wagon wheel. He ducked but it knocked his Stetson to the scuffed, hardwood floor.

Jed still firmly in tow, Beth continued to the back of the almost nonexistent dance floor, toward the "bull pit." That electronic bucking bull had been wrestled in here a couple of years ago when one of the local ranches tried to do the "dude" thing to make ends meet but failed. Tourists had always wanted to play PBR. The income had added another year to that ranch.

Then the big bull was hauled over to the bar in exchange for free drinks for the previous owners on Saturday nights, like a lifetime membership.

Flipping on the spotlights as they passed, Beth sent Jed over the back of the silent faux cowhide as she walked past. He had to bend in the middle or whack the now not-so-soft parts hard. Jed bent, head down, blood rushing in two different directions. He waited long moments for her next move. The heat from the spotlights was causing him to sweat, and he could feel rivulets running from between his shoulder blades to rest against the belt's edge on his neck. When it began to pool, a wet path ran the length of the leather and slithered along his hairline.

Beth looped the buckle into her palm, whipping the belt away. "You're a greedy bottom talking to me like that without so much as a please ma'am." The tail hit the bull next to his ear with an emphatic sound. "I know your momma instilled better manners in you. And if running off to play with the boys and beefers makes you forget them, well, I'll just be sure we freshen those up." He was staring at her legs. She wore her Wranglers like all cowboys, stacked the extra four inches deep to the top of her short Ariat boots.

When Jed saw the tail of that belt start to swing, left, right, left, right, he was reminded of her trick-roping in Jr. Rodeo and guessed she was twirling a pretty pattern. He knew he shouldn't, but he just had to look. Her feet came forward as she saw his attempt to lift his head, and that belt began raining its rhythmic blows to his shoulders and back.

Jed didn't flinch. His lifestyle had made him tough, and he had played at this before. It would take more than girlie-slapping at the back of his cotton, button-down Sunday-go-to-meetin' shirt to get him to squirm. He knew his steadiness and silence taunted Beth. He knew she liked to see a reaction from her work. And he knew that his dick had grown stiff just at the anticipation of being spanked by her.

He ground his groin against the hairy side of the faux carcass. But that wasn't doing it for him. His erection was encased in rigid indigo Wranglers. There was more chafing than coaxing of a greater excitement. A bored sigh accidentally slipped from his lips.

He realized his mistake as soon as he'd done it but not in time to stop himself. Beth reacted with speed, stripping off her own thin, dress belt to tighten it around his hands and place them behind his neck, elbows out at right angles. Then she sauntered around the other side and surprised him by deftly unbuttoning the rivet to his jeans, yanking the zipper apart with a gritty resistance, and ripping them from his ass to settle at the tops of his boots.

The well-muscled globes of his white buttcheeks stood unprotected. And though his hard-on banged up against cowhide, his balls dropped like heavy rocks to hang between his spread legs.

Beth kicked his feet as wide as the crumpled jeans would allow. She ran a shortened but sharp fingernail across one asscheek, leaving a thin red trail. He colored up so easily. Her hand reached between his legs to cup and jounce his meaty testicles. Taking a firmer hold, she drew them back through his legs to the point of stretching his scrotum. That caused Jed to lift up onto his toes.

Immediately, Beth dropped the large load and struck with leather, welting both cheeks with her first swat, lifting him slightly further until he had to land back down squarely to the bottoms of his boots once again.

"I didn't tell you to move." She stroked his flopping jewels with the scratchy side of the belt. Jed sucked his stomach in at this new twist just before the flat of the belt slapped his balls soundly.

"You may apologize."

He remained eerily silent, clenching his teeth.

The belt landed with a sting on both upper thighs, and still he was silent. Beth rained blows on his ass, making the taut globes burn bright. And still Jed had no words for her.

She thwacked him again, making the cowboy start to hump and pump against the coarse, dead hide. He knew the head of his prick would be some shade of purple, begging for release yet holding off. She shoved the tails of his shirt up until it was bunched at his shoulders to hang over the back of his head.

Beth got to work in earnest, the steady beat of the belt rhythmic. Circling the bull, she worked him from bare shoulders to ass to thighs then back. Varying the pressure but never the speed. His body tuned to the rhythm but was jarred by the change in pressure, traitorously beginning to work without him.

Jed squirmed in anticipation of each slap. His torso and ass began reaching for each oncoming blow, his toes curled as his body craved the uncertain depth of pain. He felt his control beginning to wane, his focus fade. He clenched his jaw to keep silent and heard her low laugh as his balls began to climb.

"Oh no, son. I'll have my apology and more long before those boys go home."

Her foot stepped between his calves, hooked his jeans, and dragged him back until his chest was on the bull's back and his dick and balls in midair. Feet solidly on the floor, he felt her hand pressuring the small of his back.

She trailed her fingers across the glowing stripes on his back. To anyone else it would look like he'd had enough, but he was no novice, and Beth would know his silence meant he wasn't ready to give up. She also knew how to push him where he had wanted to go.

She grabbed his hips and slammed her pelvis against his

now sensitive buttocks, insinuating fucking him up the ass. He groaned. The belt, with its hubcap-sized buckle, dropped to the wooden floor. The sound echoed within the small bar.

Beth leaned over Jed's back, feeling the heat radiating from his body, and fisted his erection. He bucked and gasped until his wits came under control enough to moan while flopping his head from side to side.

The pulsating hard-on thumped in her grasp. She stepped to his side and used her bare hand to first rub and soothe his buttocks and then slap and mar the stripes with her palm.

Now Jed tried to avoid the oncoming blows by pushing his pelvis forward into her tight grip. His head continued to rock from side to side, eyes closed, spittle leaking from his tight lips as it also leaked from his pisshole.

He would break soon. That's what he had wanted. Beth alternated between caressing his bare back and buttocks, with firm, open-handed wallops to first one reddened globe of his ass and then the other.

A single tear squeezed out of each clench-closed eye and glistened under the hot spotlight. Jed's mouth opened, the intake of air allowing his vocal chords to quietly express his erotic anguish.

Beth spanked him harder and faster until his groaning and moaning turned into recognizable words. "Fuck! No. Yes." His hands reached away from his neck, clawing with their wrists secured at the hairy hide.

She beat him soundly as she jerked him off. Jed squirmed and humped under her ministrations until his balls tightened against his body and he exploded in thick ropey stands with exhausting effort that made him sob in earnest until he eventually went slack against the big electric bull.

Beth smiled, leaned over, and cooed gently in his ear, as if to a child. She nibbled at his lobe, kissed the wetness of his cheek, and then teasingly clamped her teeth onto his jaw before rising.

Jed slid to the hardwood floor, landing soundly on his knees and sitting gingerly on the denim trapping his lower legs. He slumped forward, shoulders rounded, and leaned his head against the worn hide. His spent body heaved with his breath, hiccupping sporadically. Beth ran her hands through his hair, rubbing his head as if trying to calm a distraught child.

Gently, she loosed her belt from his wrists, replacing it around her waist in the loops of her jeans. Then she walked toward the door, flicking the spotlight off as she went. Beth plucked up the green shade, spun the sign back to "open," unlocked the bolt, and resumed her wiping of glasses behind the large mahogany bar, this time smiling and humming a country tune.

Jed, dressed and tucked, moved toward the bar as if he were saddle sore from chasing strays in the brush for a week. "Whiskey."

Beth didn't move from what she was doing.

"And, thank you, ma'am," he said.

She got him a shot that he downed in one gulp.

He dug his hand deep into a front pocket, retrieving a couple of bills. Slapping them onto the bar, Jed noticed the glint off of his wedding band. He twirled it around his ring finger with the calloused digits of his other hand. A sly grin spread across his face.

"See ya back at home."

TOYING
WITH LILY

Mike Kimera

The jeans are a deliberate act of provocation. Lily, my alleg-edly submissive, "You can do anything to me, anything at all, I'll even call you Daddy while you do it" mistress, likes to test my limits by defying me. She wants to see what I will put up with and what I will do to keep her in her place. She likes to be kept in her place.

At the moment, her place is standing in front of my chair with her hands behind her back and her head held high, waiting for me to flog, pinch, spank, and fuck her to orgasm. We both know that by now she should be naked. Instead, she has chosen to present herself wearing tight-fitting jeans and a sly smile.

True, Lily is impressively naked above the waist. She is a fully fleshed woman, short without being in any way small. Her breasts are large and heavy, and when, as now, she holds her hands behind her back, they push out almost aggressively. Her stomach is soft and flows over the cruelly tight fastening of her spray-on jeans. At any other time, I might have relaxed back into my chair and considered whether to start by using the soft calf-leather hand-lash on her belly or by suspending weighted clamps from her nipples.

But now my focus is on her jeans and the smile that accompanies them.

I could just tell her to take them off.

Or I could throw her onto the bed, wrestle them from her, maybe even cut them off her, and then raise welts on her substantial buttocks with the crop.

But that would be doing the obvious, which means I would lose the initiative. If that were to happen often enough, I would lose Lily.

I don't want to lose Lily. She makes me feel alive in a way that no one else does.

I rise out of my chair silently and lean forward until I am almost touching her.

I, of course, am fully dressed. This is the middle of the business day. A suit and tie are de rigueur. For a moment, I see myself as the Evil Victorian Headmaster about to inflict punishment on the Vulnerable Pupil. My cock salutes the image, although Lily is fourteen years younger than I am and I am stronger and larger than she is, she does not look vulnerable.

Her smile is still in place. She is daring me to do something to her. Bracing herself in pleasurable anticipation of my assault.

I push my thumbs into her jeans at each hip, grab the denim, and pull upwards until Lily is forced onto tiptoe and much of her weight is on the seam of the jeans that is riding up into her. She has the good grace to keep her unbound hands behind her back and let herself fall against my chest. The small groan that escapes her makes me smile.

I lower her until her naked feet are flat on the floor and then use her thick, wavy hair to pull her head all the way back. She is still smiling, damn her.

I push my tongue deep into her mouth. Before she can respond, I release her and step away. I want her to feel my absence for a while.

Turning my back on Lily, I face the coffee table on which she has laid out the bondage gear. It is a tradition with us that she arrives at the hotel first, bringing her toys with her. I can tell the kind of satisfaction she is seeking from the "palette" that she presents me with. I make my selection and resume my seat in front of Lily.

I'm pleased to see that she has not moved and that her tight jeans now display an impressive cameltoe. But what pleases me most is the surprise she shows when I fasten the ankle cuffs of the spreader bar over her jeans.

The whole point of the spreader bar is to keep Lily open to me, so using it when she is wearing jeans would appear to defeat the purpose. I'm sure that Lily is bursting to ask me what I intend to do, but then, of course, she would lose our game. And so she remains silent.

"Turn," I say, slapping Lily on the thigh. Legs forced wide apart, she turns awkwardly and slowly, making her breasts swing in an ungainly way that I find perversely satisfying. When she has her back to me, I rapidly put a cuff on each wrist and then fasten the cuffs together, keeping one wrist above the other. We both know that I could have done this without making her turn, but that would have been much less fun.

Lastly, I stand and fasten the collar around Lily's neck. The collar that she had set out for me covers her entire neck and has a lip that pushes upwards under her chin so that it's almost impossible for her to move her head. I know from this that Lily needs a hard session that forces the orgasms from her. Lily had already attached a leash to the front *D*-ring of the collar, inviting me to make her my bitch and drag her wherever I need her to be. She is indeed a treasure beyond price. Nevertheless, she is a defiant treasure who needs to be brought in line, a process I am now ready to start.

"It was thoughtful of you to keep your jeans on," I say, closing my hand around Lily's collared throat and forcing her back against me. "I'm sure it's a polite way of letting me know that you don't need to be fucked today."

"No!"

The word escapes before Lily can stop it. Remaining unfucked is one of the few punishments that would really make Lily suffer. To paraphrase Rhett Butler, Lily is the kind of woman who needs to be fucked often and by someone who knows how. That's one of the reasons she is here with me instead of with her loving husband: I know how.

I also control when.

"How many days has it been now, Lily?"

"Four."

I'm impressed. According to the rules, Lily is not allowed to have an orgasm for two days before we meet. It gives our meetings an edge. Four days of restraint will have honed Lily's hunger to a razor's edge. And yet she couldn't resist defying me by keeping her jeans on. Still, if Lily could move in a straight line from need to satisfaction, she wouldn't be dependent on someone like me to bind and beat her along the path to release.

"So, you haven't come in four days," I say, bringing my left hand down from Lily's throat and closing my fist around her breast, digging in my fingers hard enough to bruise the flesh. Lily stiffens at the pain, holding her breath in anticipation. "And yet you wear the jeans to keep me out."

With my right hand, I pop open Lily's jeans and pull down the zipper. Lily sighs happily and seems to be certain that she knows where my fingers will go next. She has a prominent and sensitive clitoris that reacts dramatically to being bitten or pinched or flicked hard with a fingernail. I slide my fingers in that direction, feel her arse clench against me as she prepares herself. Then I surprise her by reaching up for the leash and pulling hard until she is bent double at the waist.

Lily's size makes it an effort for her to bend like this. Her legs are tensed to take the strain, and the blood is already rushing toward her head. Her breasts hang, heavy and full. Being a generous man, I help her maintain her position by tying the end of the leash to the spreader bar.

Roughly and with some difficulty, I roll Lily's jeans down off her wide arse until her sex is exposed. I brush the tip of my finger across her slick lips and breathe in the earthy scent of her arousal. She groans. It takes all my restraint not to enter her then.

Instead, I move round in front of Lily and, reaching into my jacket, I remove a small velvet bag. She sways slightly, straining with the effort of trying to look up at me from her bent-double position. "What are you doing?"

We both know what she means is, "Why aren't you fucking me?"

I take two silver cigar-shaped cylinders out of the velvet bag. They are each about the length of my index finger but twice as thick. I hold the cylinders directly in front of Lily's face.

"These are a delightful idea, Lily. I picked them up on my last trip to Japan. An executive sex toy, just like you."

"Bastard," Lily spits at me.

"A commonly held view," I reply.

"At first they look a little like ben wa balls, don't they, Lily? I know: been there, come on that, but notice the wires at the end of each cylinder. They attach to this nifty little control that enables me to regulate the speed of their vibrations."

Lily does not look impressed. She's taken on bigger toys than this in her time.

"Size isn't everything, Lily. Persistence counts, and these things have long-life batteries. They can keep a bunny buzzing all night long."

As I talk, I slip a condom over each cylinder

"Why two condoms, you're wondering. Work it out, Lily."

Her eyes widen. "You wouldn't…"

We have been down the road less traveled from time to time, but for Lily this has been more a price she has paid than a pleasure she's sought. I want to change that. The image of Lily begging to be sodomised feeds some of my darkest hungers.

"I will, Lily. And before I untie you today, you will thank me for it."

Moving quickly, I step behind Lily to put the toys in place. I push the first cylinder all the way in. It's a bit of a struggle to get all my fingers, my thumb and the cylinder inside her, but I am very well lubed, and I persevere until I feel the cylinder touch the cervix. Lily's knees buckle slightly at the contact. But to her credit, she regains control quickly and without complaint, pushing her arse up and back, taking the rest of my hand into her up to the wrist in the process. Lily loves to be fisted. Something in the brutal power appeals to her. If I give way to her now, she will quickly fuck herself to an orgasm.

With my free hand, I slap Lily hard across the arse to bring her to a halt. Then, slowly but determinedly, I extract my hand. The wire from the cylinder hangs obscenely from Lily's pussy.

"Please," she says, her voice slightly ragged.

"The word I'm waiting for is 'Thank You.'"

"That's two words"

I smile at the fact that, even bound and fisted, Lily refuses to yield.

"Then perhaps a second cylinder is what's needed to produce them?"

Without waiting for a response, I force my cunt-slickened thumb into her arse. It's a very tight fit. "Resisting will just make this worse, Lily."

The muscle around my thumb tightens its grip.

I sigh with feigned disappointment; then I work the thumb in a slow but firm circle until the muscle relaxes a little. I slide the second condom-covered cylinder beside my thumb and push. Lily cries out at being stretched so, but I work quickly, thumb and cylinder soon swap places, and she clamps shut around the thin wire that goes to the control.

Bent over, bound, with wires dangling from both holes, Lily looks delicious. I'd like to savour the moment, but my executive slave has started swaying her hips from side to side as if she can shake the toys loose. I need to move us on. Quickly, I release the leash from the spreader bar, pull Lily upright, and then drag her jeans back up until her arse is once again clad in denim. I even manage to refasten the jeans and pull up the zip. The control hangs from the top of Lily's jeans like a tail.

"What are you doing?" Lily is not happy. She wants to be fucked, not dressed.

"Teaching you what happens when you defy me, Lily."

Then I turn on the toys.

Lily twitches like a fish on a line. I wrap one arm around her chest, pressing her back against me to keep her from falling. I've set both cylinders to high. Even covered by the jeans, I can hear their buzzy engines working away.

"You're killing me!"

"I'm helping you. But I'm a reasonable man. I'm setting the one in your cunt to low so that it's not too distracting."

The noise abates a little. Setting the toys this way will keep

Lily focused on her arse and make it less likely that she'll come quickly.

I wrap Lily's leash around my fist and then let go of her chest. Before she can regain her balance, I drag her after me toward the bed. The spreader bar makes her stagger, and it's all she can do to keep up.

Lily and I use a boutique Edwardian-themed hotel in Bloomsbury for our trysts. Part of the appeal is that the retro "gentleman's club" furniture is so bondage friendly—a bit like the gentleman's clubs were themselves, I expect. My favorite feature is the four-poster bed. Something of an anachronism for a room like this, but I'm more than willing to forgive the style lapse in favor of the practical advantages the bed offers.

I push Lily up against one of the posts at the foot of the bed and tie the leash around it at neck height. To keep her upright, I slip a line through the belt loops of her jeans and cinch it tight to the post. Then I tie the middle of the spreader bar to the dragonball foot of the bed.

Lily immediately pushes forward so that her breasts jut out on either side of the post. This is such an appealing sight that it takes me a couple of seconds to realize that Lily is humping the post, trying to get off and to distract herself from the insistent little agitator in her arse. This will not do. I put an end to her hopes by sliding an overstuffed cushion between her and the bedpost. Lily shouts her frustration in a string of curses that would make a docker blush. I do not tolerate shouting. Lily knows this. I remind her of my views by closing one hand firmly over her mouth. After a few moments the noise stops and I release her.

I'm hot, slightly out of breath, with an erection I could hammer nails with. It's time to get comfortable. I hang my jacket up, take off my tie, unbutton my collar, slip off my shoes, and climb up onto the bed in front of Lily.

My day-to-day life is filled with plans and deadlines and checklists. My time is accounted for months in advance. These sessions with Lily free me from that. In these little islands of lust and wickedness, I eschew all planning, listening only to my instincts and Lily's needs. If I can maintain my focus, my actions and her reactions can fuse into a single dance of restraint and release. Today we both have a powerful need for that release.

So far, Lily's defiance has set the scene. Now it is time for my desires to lead us in the dance.

If I listen to my blood-engorged cock, I would fuck and fuck and fuck until neither Lily nor I could move. But my cock lacks judgment. I know that my enjoyment will increase as I bring Lily closer and closer to abandoning herself, to letting go of everything except me and my will. Then I can drive us both into that moment when pleasure is all there is.

Putting conscious decision making aside, I focus on Lily.

She is slumped against the bedpost, hair sweat-damp against her forehead, breasts splayed around the phallic bedpost, legs forced wide apart by the spreader bar and arse pushed out at an inviting angle. She looks wonderful.

I kneel up on the bed and brush Lily's hair back off her forehead. She closes her eyes. Gently, I kiss each eye, letting the tip of my tongue brush lightly across her eyelids. Then I place both hands on either side of her face, close my eyes, and kiss her on the mouth.

When I pull back and open my eyes, Lily is looking at me. She is waiting calmly now. She knows the dance is about to begin.

I lean close to her, my mouth tracing the line of her jaw, my arms around her waist.

I murmur her name and feel her body relax against me. I kiss my way down her body and suck one of her nipples deep into my mouth. When I'm certain that all the tension is gone from her, I find the control hanging from her jeans and reset both cylinders to high. Lily jolts upright and tries to pull away from me. I hold her in place by biting down hard on her nipple; then I spend a delightful few moments randomly resetting the speeds of the cylinders, playing a tune with the buzzing they make and using my teeth to create a contrapuntal beat of pain in Lily's nipple. She rises up onto the balls of her feet but succeeds in not crying out. I set the cylinder in her arse to high and the one in her cunt to medium, and then I stand on the bed.

Lily is glaring up at me, mouth firmly closed as she concentrates on ignoring the sensation caused by the toys.

I smile at her and release my cock and balls from my trousers. I keep the trousers on because I enjoy the constrained freedom and because the image of naked arousal blossoming from Saville Row pinstripe pleases my sense of the absurd.

I'm now at just the right height to use Lily's mouth. At one time this would have required a ring gag. Not that Lily came to me innocent of the joys of oral sex, but she was used to "giving head," a process that allowed her complete control. I was more interested in taking than letting her give. Very little matches the satisfaction of a good face fuck. Under my tutelage, with her wrists bound behind her back and a ring gag in place, Lily learnt to surrender herself to my use. Now her throat is always available to me. All I have to do is slap her face with my erection and Lily opens her mouth wide and offers her tongue as a slipway on which to launch my violent lust.

Lily knows what I'm about to do, but she keeps her mouth defiantly closed. It takes three hard cock slaps across her cheeks before her mouth opens. I position my erection on her tongue, grasp her jaw and the back of her head, and force myself into her mouth. The angle is not the easiest, and my cock is proving itself inflexible, but I manage three firm strokes, the last of which gets

almost all of me into her mouth. I hold her head in place until I
see the tears forming in her eyes. Then I pull out.

"Be a good girl for Daddy," I say, pulling Lily's head back so
she is looking up at me. "Beg me to sodomise you."

Lily is still getting her breath back, so she shakes her head
firmly and waits to see what I will do next.

This time it takes four cock slaps before Lily's mouth opens.
I slip my index fingers into either side of her mouth and use my
thumbs to push my balls past her lips.

"Work your tongue, Lily. Suck like you mean it. I know
you've had the practice."

Lily's eyes narrow, but she works my balls nonetheless. The
sensation itself is not particularly exciting, although seeing my
erection rest on Lily's face while she struggles to please me is
entertaining. As with so many pleasures, context is everything.
In this case the context is set by the fact that it is not my balls
that Lily has been practicing on.

I think it's only fair that, if you are going to fuck another man's
wife, he should get some benefit from it. Alan, Lily's husband, is
a man of simple sexual needs who, over the two years of my association with Lily, has found his sex life becoming more complex.
First, I had Lily habituate him to letting her film their fucking.
She told him it turned her on. True enough in its way. She has
come many times while replaying the film on the state-of-the-art
LCD screen the hotel thoughtfully provides. I like to try to beat
a come out of her before her husband's onscreen performance
ends with him collapsed on top her. Initially, this didn't give me
a lot of time, but I usually managed it.

After awhile, I had Lily insist on being on top, facing toward
the camera when they fucked. I'd grown profoundly tired of
watching Alan's arse; the sight of Lily bumping and grinding and
pulling at her breasts was a decided improvement. It also had the

benefit of making the fucking last long enough for me to do a more thorough job of beating Lily during the playback. Besides, with Lily facing the camera, she could mouth "Thank you, Daddy," before each sticky dismount. It's our way of sharing.

Recently, I've spiced things up a bit by phoning Lily before each session with Alan and telling her how I want her fucked. At my bidding, Alan has been introduced to the delights of having his balls sucked and his arsehole rimmed while Lily jacks him off onto her tits. Alan never lasts long, but he is extremely grateful. Lily, on the other hand, finds these sessions very frustrating. When Alan is happily asleep, I call her and make her fuck herself for me in front of the camera while Alan's drying cum puckers the skin on her breasts.

Now Lily is sucking my balls when she would rather be fucking. I'm sure the message is not lost on her. When my balls are wet, I pull them out of her mouth but leave them resting against her cheek.

"Ask Daddy to ream your arse, Lily, there's a good girl."

"Please, Daddy," Lily says, "Fuck me hard and deep."

I smile. Progress.

"But use my cunt. It's wet and it aches for you. Please, Daddy."

Not enough progress. Time to change tactics.

I climb down from the bed, my cock swaying absurdly in front of me, and set to work on detaching Lily from the bedpost. Leaving her hands cuffed behind her back and the spreader bar in place, I wrap the leash around my fist and pull her roughly down onto the bed so that she's lying on her back with her legs spread.

She can't help but grin as she bounces on the bed. Lily is anticipating getting fucked. I'm anticipating taking her breath away.

It seems the constant stimulation from the toys has had an effect; the crotch of Lily's jeans has been darkened with moisture. Instinctively, I lower my head to investigate. Lily lifts her hips, offering herself to me. Now it's my turn to grin.

I place my hands on her thighs and push them even further apart. Quickly and without warning, I bite down hard on Lily's mound. She thrashes beneath me, too shocked even to scream. I bite a second time and she stiffens, back arched. The third bite does it; Lily's first orgasm rides her. When the shaking stops, I grab the spreader bar and use it to force her to bend her legs until her knees are pressing into her breasts. I'm bent over her, inches from her face, tying the leash to the spreader bar so that she will remain folded, when her eyes open.

"You BIT me."

There is as much surprise as anger in her voice.

"Yes."

"THREE times"

Indignation seems to be losing out to incredulity. I finish the knot that will keep Lily bent double, kiss her forcefully on the mouth, and say, "It seemed like the right number."

"You are a sick, twisted freak."

"And your point is?"

"Fuck me. Fuck me right now. Please."

I stand up and start to undress, slowly, carefully folding each item as it is removed.

"Come ON." Lily says, rocking a little, testing the strength of the knot that holds her.

I still have my trousers and shoes on. I will not tolerate being hurried.

I grab the spreader bar and push down until it rests quite firmly against Lily's neck. "You will be quiet now, Lily," I say. My voice is level and calm and all the more menacing for that.

"You will not speak until after I have fucked you."

I can see that Lily wants to ask a question, but she restrains herself.

"Good girl," I say.

I stand where Lily can see me while I finish undressing. Her eyes never leave me.

When I move to the coffee table to pick up what I need, she loses sight of me. She doesn't see the knife until I climb back on the bed.

We both know the knife is very sharp. We keep it that way in case I need to cut through any bonds in a hurry. I run the blade across my thumb. Blood blossoms bright and fast. I push my thumb into Lily's mouth. She doesn't need to be told to suck.

"You should have taken the jeans off, Lily," I say, running the knife flat along her breast until the blunt side of the blade presses against her nipple. Lily stops sucking. As far as I can tell, she stops breathing.

I withdraw my still-bleeding thumb and move the knife between Lily's legs, placing the tip against the seam of her jeans. She closes her eyes but does not scream or try to move. I'm proud of her.

Lily still has her eyes closed when I put the knife down on the bed and start to manhandle her jeans. It isn't easy, but I manage to get them undone and drag them down her legs until they are bunched at her knees and her arse is exposed.

Lily's sex is soaked. The rich, earthy smell of her arousal floods my senses, making me salivate with need. I bend closer, breathing her in. Only then do I notice the cylinder control hanging out of her. I'd almost forgotten about them in all the excitement. I reach down and turn them both off.

Lily opens her eyes and grins at me.

On her back, bent double, legs forced apart by the spreader

bar that is still tied to her collar, toys in each sweat-slickened hole, Lily is an invitation to wickedness.

I'm not in the mood for finesse. I tug the cylinder out of Lily's cunt easily. The one in her arse takes more work, but it's clear that her muscles are much more relaxed than they were.

Lily is looking at me intently. My guess is she's willing me to fuck her cunt. My focus is a little lower, but the angle is not quite right. I slide my hand, palm up, into Lily's sopping sex, clamp my thumb on her clit, and lift her just a little.

Keeping my hand in her, I position my cock against her arse-hole and push. God, she is tight. The head of my cock squeezes its way in. Her arse ring clamps on my shaft, but I keep pushing until I am all the way in.

All I want now is to fuck. Ignoring her protests and pleas, I pull my hand out of her and position myself for maximum leverage by closing my fists around her breasts and letting her take my full weight. Then I let loose all my control, and I fuck as hard and as fast and for as long as I can. I'm aware that Lily is making some kind of noise, but for once I'm not listening. I'm nothing but sweat, and muscle and heat and friction until finally, deep inside her, I find release.

When I come back to myself, all tension, all sense of purpose has left me. Still inside her, I work impatiently to release Lily's ankle cuffs from the spreader bar. I throw it aside and let myself collapse onto her.

"You can speak now, Lily," I say, softly in her ear.

For a moment she says nothing, just wraps her legs around me. Then, in a voice that oozes contentment, she says, "Thank you, Daddy."

TURNAROUND

A. D. R. Forte

I tell Mrs. Bryce-Graham, known to her friends as just Anna, thank you. She shushes me, tells me she's glad to help, and hangs up. I put a check next to her name on the donation list and smile gratefully at the promised amount.

I've known Anna for more than ten years now, but I'm still a little in awe of her. Her very important job, her very extensive knowledge of recipes for anything and everything, her very elegant clothes that go so well with her very stylish haircut. Her unfailing, unpretentious generosity. If princesses existed in the modern world and held poli-sci degrees and raised model children, that would be Anna.

Not like me sitting around in my sweats, grateful my kids are at their grandmother's for a week so I can get caught up on the piles of tests I have yet to grade, on the overdue deadlines to the magazine I supposedly freelance for, on the Humane Society fundraising I promised to do, and maybe, just maybe, even clean this mess of a house. I shuffle some books and a plate of toast

crumbs aside and wince at the thought of Anna's always spotless
kitchen. Why is spring break only one week?

The phone rings and, without looking, I pick it up and click
the talk button, still contemplating the woefully short donation
list. I put the receiver to my ear and forget to say hello in the
shock of hearing Anna's voice. Except... is that Anna?

Yes. Muffled as if the phone is in her purse, background driving
noise like before, but still recognizable. Except... except...

"...swear to you, Sir. I haven't." The words make no sense,
not from my friend, the *Ladies Home Journal* poster child. I
hear rustling and then a thump as if phone and purse and all
have fallen or been dropped on the floor.

Sounding distant, a male voice replies, one that I recognize
with another jolt of shock as David Bryce-Graham's—only like
I've never heard it before, deep and dangerous and tinged with
lazy amusement.

"I don't believe you, Anna."

I hear a stifled sound. A feminine moan through clamped
lips. Like me, when Clint and I are fucking and trying not to be
loud. I know what I'm hearing, but I refuse to comprehend.

More rustling.

Then: "These give you away," David says, laughter in his
voice. And even more dangerously: "You have been thinking
about her, darling. You want to fuck her, don't you?"

My brain is so busy reeling from the idea of hearing David
Bryce-Graham using the f-word like that to his wife, to *Anna*,
that I almost miss her very soft, "Yes, Sir."

"Hmm. That's what I thought." A pause. "You know, I think
I'm going to have to pull over."

"No, Sir!"

"Oh yes." He laughs.

My conscience screams at me to hang up, hang up now. I

shouldn't be hearing this, I don't want to be hearing this! My cheeks are burning, I want to crawl under the table and hide, and already I know I'm never going to be able to look either of them in the eye again. Not without embarrassment and guilt written all over my face.

But instead of hanging up, I fumble for the Mute button, reluctant to take the phone away from my ear for even a moment. Once I'm sure the mute is on, I press the button for Speaker and sit listening to the purr of the engine until there's silence.

He's made good on his threat; they've stopped.

A sound that I guess is seatbelts being taken off.

"What if someone comes by?" she asks, sounding almost like the educated, unruffled woman I know.

"There's nobody for ten miles around but cows, love."

"But..."

"Out of the car *now*, Anna!"

I jump and put my hand over my mouth, and I can almost feel her heart hammering just as hard as mine as she opens the door. I wonder if it's fear for her or pleasure. Or both. Some ashamed little part of me longs to know.

I hear shoes scrunch on gravel.

"It's cold," she protests, voice fainter as she gets out of the SUV, and I hold my breath so that I don't miss a word.

"A hot little slut like you shouldn't mind," David says. "Now take your jacket off and turn around."

With her delicate frame, Anna doesn't like the cold and it's in the 50s outside. I shiver for her.

"Here's good enough." His tone is forgiving, just a little, and his voice sounds closer. "Put your hands on the doorframe. That's right."

Vague rustles and movement. Her voice in small sounds of denial or maybe excitement.

"You are lovely like this."

Like this? Chewing on my thumbnail, I'm dying to know what "this" is. I picture her shoulder-length, brown hair loose because she usually wears it down if she's not at work.

"It's so cold, David," she says, voice shaking. Pleading.

"Your own fault darling. If you hadn't been wearing that damned bra, you wouldn't have had to take it off."

Oh god, he's got her top off, and her bra. I squeeze my eyes shut and try not to let imagination color in the picture of her round breasts bare, nipples puckered from the cold. Is he touching them? Playing with her?

I fidget on the smooth wooden seat of the kitchen chair.

"May I keep my skirt on, Sir?" she asks, not daring to hope. I hold my breath and listen again.

"Yes, you may. But you're going to pull those wet little panties down... that's far enough... Now lift your skirt up higher... That's it. Ass up. Stick it out like a good slut... Perfect. Hands on the doorframe... Good."

I give up. Eyes closed, I can see her standing there on some deserted country road, holding onto the passenger-side doorway of the Escalade, naked from the waist up, panties around her knees, gooseflesh on her arms and legs and bare ass, David's tall frame standing behind her to shelter her a little from the wind. Commanding her.

This is so beyond all that's wrong and unacceptable, but it's too late to back out now.

I hear David's voice, cajoling, reprimanding.

"What do you think Kellie would say if she could see you like this?"

I want to yell "What?" at the top of my voice. I stare at the phone, squeezing the receiver so hard it's in danger of slipping out of my grasp. Me? What do *I* have to do with this? It can't...

he couldn't have meant...

"You'd like her to, wouldn't you?"

I don't know what reply she gives him, and I don't want to know. I don't. I don't!

David laughs.

"Such a bad girl, having such dirty thoughts about her friends." He does something to her and she moans. "What else would you like Kellie to do, darling?"

Oh god. No. NO!

She doesn't answer and I'm thanking all the angels and saints when I hear the first slap. She gasps and I jump. Then another slap. The sounds are remote but unmistakable.

The sound of a palm hitting flesh in the only logical place he can possibly be hitting her. *This*... this is too much. My brain should have shorted out a long time ago. What's wrong with me? Why am I still listening?

Because I want to know what she wants me to do?

He says, "I'm still waiting for an answer."

"Please..."

"Answer me, slut. What do you want Kellie to do to you?"

"Nothing, Sir."

Another slap, louder than before, and she cries out sharply. I wince.

"Nothing?"

"Nothing! I want... I want to..." She's sobbing to get the words out as he slaps her ass again and again.

"What, Anna?" Slap. "What filthy little fantasies has your pretty mind conjured up? I want to know."

"K... Kellie... I want to lick her cunt. I want her... to use me. While I'm tied."

I can't hear what he says. Approval, I suppose. Doesn't matter because I'm dying of shame. My hand holding the phone is sweating, and I'm shaking like one of my fourth-graders caught cheating on a test.

I'm fighting not to imagine the scene she's just described. Her sleek, soft hair falling on my open thighs. Her pretty, pouty lips on my clit, tongue licking at my wetness. Her hands *tied* behind her back. Something out of the porn sites I've found on Clint's laptop and secretly stared at, dry mouthed and wide eyed.

But as hard as I fight my conscious thought, my body betrays me. My clit is throbbing, and the seam of my pants rubs me like a knowing finger as Anna continues her confession. As David delivers her penance, slap by slap.

"I want her to come on my face. I want to hear her moan."

"The way you moan for me?"

She replies with one, and he slaps her hard. She cries out again.

"What else?"

"I... I want to finger her. I want her to fuck me."

"Slut." He laughs. "You want Kellie's pretty fingers to fuck you? Like this?"

She groans and gasps and I can imagine his fingers plunging in and out of her dripping pussy. Rubbing her clit and her reddened ass.

"Yes. Yes oh god, please!"

She's so close. I know it. I can feel her rising, the throbbing in her clit and her belly. Then he slaps her again. She groans. Pain and pleasure.

"David please!"

"What is it, slut?"

"Please. Please. I need to come!" She's begging.

"You know the only way you get to come when you're being punished."

"Yes," she sobs. "Yes."

Silence.

I put the phone down and put both hands over my mouth. Shivering, like her, I wait. Except that she knows her fate, which must make it so much worse. Is she thinking about me? Imagining me touching her as David punishes her?

I tell myself I'm sick for the powerful, excited flood of feeling between my legs as I think of being treated in kind for my thoughts about her. For my pride and perversion in knowing Anna—beautiful, perfect Anna—wants me. Like that.

At the crack of renewed slaps, I jump. My thighs tense inward, rubbing pants seam against clit as I hear her scream. Blow after blow, and at every one she gasps and I can hear her moaning, crying in earnest now.

Slowly my lust- and shock-addled brain puts it together. He's not slapping her, not with that rhythmical swish and hiss and thwack. He's spanking her with something. A belt? Or something worse? My stomach thrills cold.

I can see her writhing in the doorway, the shock of each blow filling her clit, filling her cunt with painful vibration. Closer and closer, her ass pure pain but her clit sweet throbbing agony. Her cries become strangled, breathless. I know she's there.

And then the unbearable rhythm stops. Ragged panting. Perhaps he's kissing her now, caressing her breasts or maybe her ass. Milking the last of her orgasm from her abused flesh.

She whispers a word. I think it sounds like David.

Right now, I'd give anything to see them like that. Master and lady fair.

Fingers shaking, I reach out and press talk once more. The LCD winks out and the silence of my own ordinary house fills my ears. I'm still shaking, torn with desire and the urge to pull my sweatpants down and finish myself off.

What feels like hours is barely a minute before I give in. I wriggle out of the pants and I've just kicked off my own wet panties when I hear a sound behind me. Heart beating loud enough to burst my eardrums, I spring to my feet and turn around. Clint walks into the room. Face red, jeans bulging deliciously.

"How much did you hear?" I blurt.

"Enough," he says after a minute, after he's looked me over. My nipples poking through the baggy sweatshirt, my bare legs and bare pussy, fragrant with desire and the evidence of my guilty voyeur's pleasure. I've never needed a fuck so badly before, but he makes no move to undo his fly.

And suddenly I wonder.

Clint grins at me, a really wicked grin.

"Turn around," he says.

FLICK CHICKS

Allison Wonderland

From my place on the chaise, I examine my lover, observing her primping ritual at the vanity table. Sitting on the cushion, clad in sheer chiffon chemise and sugar cone cup bra, Mae looks like she belongs to a different era. An era of starlets and glamour girls and pinup queens. When passersby pass Mae by, they often pause for a moment, expecting the scenery to segue from Technicolor to black-and-white.

Mae plucks her lipstick from the tabletop, swivels the tube, glides the wedge along her lips, creating a circle of crimson. Next are her eyes, the lashes extended with mascara, the lids anointed with gold powder. Glitzy gold, like the statuettes dispensed at the Academy Awards. Now the coiffure. Mae's hair is her crowning glory. Jean Harlow blonde with Bettie Page bangs. She unrolls the pistachio pinsetters, arms raised and bent at the elbows, resembling a ballerina poised in pirouette. When she is finished, she scrutinizes her reflection in the mirror. Sliding her glasses onto her nose, Mae peers through the cat's-eye frames of the spectacles, studying the visage of a vixen.

"Let's get cracking."

Mae jerks at the sound of my voice. She hates it when I do that. Frown crimping her lips, she turns in my direction, sees me reclining on the lounge, limbs limp, head cushioned by a fluffy round pillow. Pinched between my fingers is a vinyl riding crop, its shaft tapping against the veneer of the maple wood.

Mae rises to her feet, saunters over to the settee, her slender heels stabbing the parquet floor. "What's this?" she demands, fingering the fabric of my brassiere.

My attire is nearly identical to Mae's. Garish garters engird my thighs. Black satin gloves conceal the flesh from forearms to fingertips. Nylon stockings cleave to my calves, travel to my toes, and then disappear inside shiny black stilettos. However, unlike Mae and her missile cups, I have opted for a simple black bra.

"What's wrong?" I pout, feigning innocence.

Mae seizes a strap, stretching it away from my shoulder. Upon release, it snaps against my skin, evoking a savory synthesis of pain and pleasure.

"I don't like the bullet style," I assert, guiding my body into a sitting position. "It looks like something that belongs on the obstacle course at driving school."

"You—" Mae starts, but this is as far as she gets. I watch as her gaze strays to the implement in my hand, watch as her eyes glide along the shiny black switch.

"I know what you're thinking," I drawl, pressing the tip of the whip into Mae's shoulder, eliciting titters and trembles.

Mae settles onto my lap, the lacy accents of her scanties tickling my thighs. "Oh?" she queries, digits stroking the curve of my hip.

My limbs quiver at the contact. "You're thinking—"

"I can speak for myself, thank you," Mae affirms, and snatches the whip from my grip. She hops off my lap, strides to the tripod assembled in the center of the room.

I watch as my lover adjusts the camera. "Well?"

"Hmm?" Mae murmurs, lips pursed in concentration.

"What are you thinking?"

She laughs, looks up at me. "I was thinking," she says, "that it's time to spank your fanny, Dani." Mae's tone is flippant, almost nonchalant, but her expression belies the inflection in her voice.

I study my lover's eyes behind their tilted frames. The irises glimmer, incandescent, like a theatre marquee.

In a matter of minutes, we will be transported to the 1950s, recreating the tame but tantalizing stag films that featured the three *B*'s: bondage, backsides, and Bettie Page. Mae and I own a production company, creating erotic films for the nostalgically inclined. We work both behind and in front of the camera. Not out of necessity, although finances are a factor, but by choice.

A year ago, however, when Mae first proposed the idea, I chafed at her suggestion. Porn? She wanted to make *porn*?

The word reeked of peep shows and peeping toms.

I envisioned films with such titles as *Rock around the Cock* and *A Tale of Two Titties*.

I envisioned our audience—men clad in flimsy beige trench coats, sweat drenching their brows.

I imagined—

Here, Mae interrupted my imaginings, first with a kiss, then with a compromise. "You'll only have one costar," she promised. "Me. It'll be just the two of us." Then she added, thinking that she could change my mind by changing words, "And we won't really be making porn. We'll be making...period pieces."

Still, I remained skeptical.

"Just the two of us," Mae reiterated. "And perhaps some equestrian equipment…"

Inevitably, I warmed up to the idea, because the more I deliberated, the more alluring the proposition became. It began to intrigue me—the thought of someone looking, desiring from a distance, aching to touch yet not being able to. And so I agreed, and *Cup of Tease* was born.

"You ready?" Mae inquires, angling the lens toward the settee. On celluloid, the mint green upholstery will be converted to a grainy gray.

"Picture you upon my knee," I croon. "Just tease for two and two for tease."

Mae's smile segues into a smirk. "Actually, Dani," she says, tapping the riding crop against her calf, "you'll be on my knee today, remember?"

She gestures for me to lie down. I take direction well. Maneuvering my body into repose, I melt into the cushion, the satin fabric conforming to the contours of my figure.

Mae pushes the record button.

Action.

Expelling a yawn, I pretend to stir from slumber, extending my arms behind my head, arching my back like a feline stretching after a nap. I ball my fists, twist them in front of my eyes, back and forth, to and fro.

I look straight into the camera and gasp, expanding the oval of my mouth, widening the circumference of my eyes, as though I have just been caught unawares. But soon my surprise transitions into curiosity. I wave at the lens, fluttering my fingers, batting my eyelashes.

The flaunting and flashing is next. I contort my body into various cheesecake poses—lying on my belly with legs flexing, lying on my back with legs kicking.

I rise to my feet, pucker my lips, smack them together, blowing invisible kisses to the camera. I am cheeky and coquettish, wholesome yet wanton.

I begin to wriggle. I swivel and shimmy and sashay, my body undulating like a Slinky. When I dance, I dance for Mae and Mae alone. I watch her watch me from behind the tripod. She slides her glasses down the bridge of her nose, revealing her eyes, sienna swirls of desire.

In the next moment, Mistress Mae enters the frame, switch clenched in her grip, scowl tugging at her lips. Mistress deplores dancing. Mae's gloved hand wraps around my arm, her fingers singeing my flesh. I pout, I whimper, I grovel. But to no avail. Mistress drags me to the settee, flings my flailing body onto her lap. My resistance is a ruse. In reality, the thought of the forthcoming flogging kindles my arousal. I can feel a puddle forming inside my panties, the sticky cream clinging to the fabric.

Mae's palm connects with my backside. I yelp, thrashing my legs in a semblance of suffering. Mistress makes contact again. My feet and fists pummel the air in fictitious agony. I writhe against her lap, the material between my legs smearing nectar onto my mound. It feels warm and waxy, like butterscotch.

Mae yanks my panties from my bottom, exposing the cheeks and cleavage of my rump. I twist my head to look at her. She winks at me, the corners of her mouth pointed upwards. So smug, so sultry. Mae's fingers graze my flesh. She is tender at first, stroking me the way a guitarist strums the strings of her instrument, lulling me into a false sense of security.

The blow stings, like a slap across the face, only not so unpleasant.

Then harder. But not hard enough. The honey hue of my skin camouflages the strawberry shade of the marks, and she has to hit me harder for them to be visible.

The next strike is hard enough to brand me with her hand, to leave an indelible imprint on my flesh. I wait for more, expect it, thirst for it. But it doesn't come. I mewl, craning my neck to see why she has stopped. Mistress raises the riding crop, swishes it in front of my face. The punishment isn't over; it is merely entering the next phase. I wince, displaying a façade of fear.

Mae's tongue touches the tip of the whip, tracing, stroking, the way she licks the frosting off a cupcake. My hips buck, betraying the illusion. Mistress shoves my head back down, her fingers tangling in my hair, her nails scratching my scalp. I hiss at the sensations, clenching my eyes shut.

Three whops land in quick succession. The pleasure zips from my posterior to my pussy, the way a spark surges along the fuse of a stick of dynamite. My panties are saturated, the juices creeping along the edges, soaking the chiffon trim, en route to Mae's thighs. She shifts, lifts her leg slightly, pressing it into my cunt.

The switch sears my bottom. Pangs of pleasure whisk through my body, overwhelming my senses. Another twinge, another twitch. My muscles ache, but I disregard the pain. I can feel a rectangular welt beginning to take shape, a welcome complement to the impressions of Mae's hands.

I have lost count of the number of times the crop has made contact with my rump. I no longer have the energy to engage in such useless tasks as tallying thrashings. Instead, I invest my energy into relieving the unceasing ache between my legs.

Lids screwed shut, lashes scraping the skin beneath my eyes, I flail my limbs at full throttle. Gyrate my pelvis, grind against Mae's thigh, smearing my juices on the alabaster skin.

To all outward appearances, I am a woman ensnared in the throes of agony. Yet while my convulsions convey misery, Mistress knows better. Mistress cannot be fooled. Mistress knows when I come.

Soon after, Mae taps my bottom with her hand, indicating that the whipping is over. I rise to my feet, bringing my hands to my backside, a pretense of protection. Mae brandishes the whip in my face, a threat of future floggings if I'm naughty again. I bow my head in deference and pout, the corners of my mouth sagging like wilted violets. Mistress smiles, pleased with the effect of the punishment. Gently, she tugs my panties back into place, concealing my bruised bottom.

I watch as she exits, no longer visible in the frame. She retreats behind the camera, deactivates the device, and returns to my side. Smiling, she reaches behind me, squeezes my cheeks. I flinch, teeth nearly puncturing my lip. The flesh is throbbing now, but the pleasure is worth the pain, the pain worth the pleasure. Mae slides a hand inside the elastic band of my panties. Her fingers soothe the soreness, her touch tender and hesitant, as if I am made of glass.

"Next time, I'll handle you with kid gloves," Mae teases, pressing her lips to mine.

"Then you'll have to find a new costar," I threaten, reciprocating the kiss.

"Picture you upon my knee," Mae croons. "Just tease for two and two for tease."

"Actually, Mae," I say, and snatch the whip from her grip, "I've already been upon your knee. You, however, have not yet been upon mine."

Mae glances at the camera.

"Is there enough film?" I ask.

"Yes," she answers, tracing the outline of the welt on my backside. "Let's not do a sequel, though. Let's just pick up where we left off."

I nod, contemplating Mistress' comeuppance, deliberating where to stand since sitting is out of the question.

"What should we call this film?" Mae inquires, brow furrowed in thought.

I remove her hands from my body, stroll toward the vanity, deposit the riding crop between the perfume bottle and the lotion dispenser. I scan the table, surveying the various accoutrements. The hairbrush catches my eye. It is the paddle kind, its square head large and expansive. "We should call it," I begin, curling my fingers around the handle, "*Bottoms Up.*"

EQUILIBRIUM

Anna Black

Helen Carter slowly sipped her cup of hot white tea. Wrapped securely in a blanket, she was re-reading one of her favorite erotic novels. This was how she spent nearly all of her nights. At home. Alone. Lost in the fantasy of a life she'd never have. She wondered sometimes if people could sense the longings in her. The desire to balance the dark cravings she had in bed with the persona she presented to the outside world. To find a sense of equilibrium.

She squirmed against the couch as she came to an especially luscious scene in which the Viscount Letchford finally had his ward, the innocent Lady Margaret Claypool, across his knees; her petticoats hiked up around her slender waist, her pantaloons rucked down around her trim ankles, her pert bottom anxiously awaiting the first smack of his autocratic hand.

The apartment intercom buzzed.

Sighing, Helen set the book aside, rose from the couch, and went over to press the talk button. "Yes?" She hoped the door attendant wasn't able to hear the aggravation in her voice. He was, after all, only doing his job.

"Sorry to disturb you, Ms. Carter." Damn. Apparently he had. "But there's a gentleman here with a package for you."

"A package?" She frowned. At this time of the night? "From whom?"

Helen heard a muffled conversation in the background. Then the door attendant's voice. "Everett Lyles."

Her heart thumped hard in her chest.

"Shall I send him up?"

"Yes, please."

She crossed her arms over her breasts. It had been a week since her presentation to Everett Lyles. As an architect at the firm that Lyles had contacted as a possible designer for the mansion he was planning to build, Helen had been given the assignment—as the firm's president had put it—to woo him.

A wealthy expatriate from England, Lyles had been tall, impeccably dressed, and shockingly gorgeous, with an equally gorgeous accent that had not only sounded upper-class and moneyed but, by the end of Helen's presentation, had left her panties damp and her nipples hard.

But her presentation had been for naught. As she was leaving this evening, the company's president informed her that Lyles had elected to go with another firm. An outcome that he let her know—in that elegantly silky but unquestionably pissed-off tone of his—had greatly disappointed him.

As usual, Helen had suspected that his disappointment had been less with Lyles' decision and more with her. So, as she waited for the deliveryman to come up to her apartment, she wondered, with no small degree of irritation, what the man, who had come close to possibly getting her fired, could be sending her.

There was a knock. Helen peered through the peephole and

saw a man who did not look anything at all like a deliveryman. If anything, he looked more like a chauffeur. She opened the door.

"Miss Carter?"

"Yes?

He handed her a large white box. She took it, awkwardly cradling it in her arms. The man gave a slight nod and then turned and walked down the hall to the elevator.

Helen closed and locked the door. She took the box to the couch, sat down, and opened it. Tissue paper hid the contents. On top rested an envelope. She took out a sheet of heavy, expensive paper. The handwriting was bold and masculine. As she read, she frowned, but the beating of her heart sped up.

This coming Friday she was to be outside her apartment at 7:45 p.m. exactly. Carlton, whom the note described as the man who had dropped off the box, would be waiting for her in a limo. He would drive her to the east side of the city. Helen recognized the address. One of the firm's clients had lived there before he moved into his ten-bedroom mansion outside the city. The address screamed money.

The rest of the note instructed her to wear what was inside the box. Helen placed the note on the couch. She turned back to the box and pushed aside the tissue paper. She stared at the contents.

Red silk blouse.

Long black skirt.

High-heeled, ruby-red, fuck-me shoes.

Black sheer stockings and lace garters.

And a black mesh lingerie bodysuit embroidered with red roses, a push-up bra, and a thong that would leave the cheeks of her buttocks exposed.

As Helen stared at the clothes, she noted that something had been slipped in between the skirt and the blouse: a photograph of a bearded Victorian man spanking the plump, bare bottom of a young woman.

Blood rushed through her body and warmed her cheeks. How had he known? How had Lyles fathomed the most secret places of her heart in the short span of time she had spent with him?

In Helen's mind she saw his face. Those fallen-angel features. That firm, sensuous mouth. And the way he had sat during her presentation; the essence of cool, controlled masculinity.

"Lower the lights."

She had been adjusting the focus on the projector. At the sound of his voice Helen had looked over at him. They were the first words—other than his clipped greeting to her—that he said that day in the conference room. And he had spoken them with a meticulous authority that she sensed would not tolerate any dispute on her part.

"Excuse me?" she'd said even as a dark thrill pulsed through her.

Lyles had made a slight gesture with his chin towards the screen on which her slide presentation was projected. "I can't see that. The lights. Lower them."

Helen had walked to the light switch on the wall, feeling intensely aware of her body; the pivoting of her hips under her slim skirt, the whisper of her stockings as her thighs crisscrossed, the rise and fall of her breasts as she breathed.

She'd lowered the lights and then looked over at Lyles, who had inclined his head in approval. But his handsome features were otherwise aloof. For the next half hour, as she had gone over her presentation, he had sat unmoving, his long fingers steepled before his dimpled chin, his sea-green eyes gleaming in the low lights of the room.

When she had finished, he'd asked no questions, voiced no concerns, raised no issues. He had only thanked her for the presentation and had taken her business card when she offered it to him. Then, today, had come the news that he had chosen another firm to design his house.

Now there was this. A blatant invitation to come to his luxury apartment and allow him to indulge her most secret fantasy. Helen looked at the photo, and her cunt moistened as she imagined some proper, straitlaced Victorian vigorously spanking her ass for some minor transgression on her part.

Then she imagined Everett Lyles doing the punishing.

She shook her head to clear her thoughts and focused back on the clothes. How did he know she would even wear such things? Somehow she suspected there were other things about her that he knew. Just from looking at her. Watching her. Listening to her.

She picked up the note and read it again.

7:45 p.m. This Friday.

She put the note down and picked up the blouse. She looked at the label, not surprised to see the shirt was exactly her size.

Helen stood in front of the door to Lyles' apartment. She was nervous, but she had come this far. There was no sense in backing out now.

She took a deep breath and knocked.

Lyles opened the door and gestured for her to enter. She did so, her heels clicking on the hardwood floor of the foyer.

"Come," he said. "I have something to show you."

Helen followed him to the wall nearest to the large windows. Outside was a spectacular view of the city's skyline. He stopped in front of a built-in cabinet and pulled open a huge drawer. Inside, carefully stored, was a collection of assorted spanking paraphernalia: paddles, whips, belts, rods, canes. A miscellany of instruments to be used for both pain and pleasure.

Lyles picked up a strap of leather, the end of which was split into two tails. "This is called a tawse. It's from Scotland and was originally used to discipline students in school." He turned it over in his hands. "This is a Lochgelly Taswe."

"Lochgelly?"

"Yes. This one's a medium weight one. I have others in London. I'll have them sent over when my home is completed."

Helen frowned. "Why didn't you choose our firm? Was it something I said or did? Or didn't do?"

"What do you think?"

She shrugged.

Lyles ran the straps of the tawse through his long, elegant fingers. "You blame yourself?"

Helen thought about it. The firm's president had not been subtle in letting her know that he considered it some flaw on her part that had kept her from nailing what would have been a very big client.

"Well?" Lyles prompted. There was a tinge of impatience in his voice.

"Yes, I failed."

"And were you punished?"

She gave him a sharp look. "Punished?"

His green eyes gazed deeply into hers. "Chastised for your failure. Disciplined for your malfeasance."

"My boss was not happy."

"Obviously. But did he punish you?" Lyles' voice bore down on the word *punish*.

"No, of course not."

His lips furled into a slight smile. "Would you like to be?"

"What?"

"Punished."

Helen licked her lips. "Is that why you invited me here?"

"You didn't answer my question," he said.

She glanced at the tawse in his hand. Her breath caught in her throat.

"With that?"

"If you like." He looked at the other objects in his collection. "I have my preferences, but…" He held the tawse by its handle and flicked it through the air. "I do like my Lochgelly."

"And those who have"—she gestured at the tawse, her pulse beating in her throat—"been under it?"

The edges of his lips curled up. "There have been no complaints."

"Then, yes. With that."

He pointed to a pole near the wall. "Go over there."

Helen went over to the pole. Lyles followed her.

"Take off your skirt."

Helen did so, stepping carefully out of it in order not to snare the hem on her high-heeled shoes. There was no place nearby for her to put it.

"Drop it," Lyles ordered.

She did so, conscious of her bare buttocks and the thong of her bodysuit riding up the crack of her ass.

"Turn around and take hold of the pole."

She did as he instructed.

"Are you ready?"

Helen swallowed and nodded.

His large, cool hand gently cupped one cheek of her bare ass. She heard his slow, even breath, smelled his scent, his cologne woodsy and decidedly male. She stared at the wall opposite her and slowly closed her eyes.

As if that were the signal—although she knew Lyles could not see her face—she heard the whisk of the tawse as he moved it through the air.

The leather straps lashed across her skin, and she shuddered, her hands gripping the pole, her cunt puckering, hot tears stinging the edges of her eyes.

A moment passed. Then Lyles flogged her ass again. And again. And again. After the fifth lash, he demanded she beg for the next one.

She did.

And for each and every one thereafter.

As the blows continued to fall across her quivering buttocks, Helen pushed her breasts against the pole and rubbed her stiff nipples along it. She wriggled her ass each time Lyles struck her, which caused the thong to ride up between the lips of her sex, rubbing steadily against her clitoris. The thin fabric grew slick with her wetness.

She soon lost count of the strokes of the tawse.

"More?" Lyles' voice was heavy and thick, like the honey that had pooled at the base of her belly.

Helen leaned against the pole, her breath fast and harsh. She rubbed up and down it like a cat along its master's leg. She slowly lowered her head.

"One more. Please."

The leather straps of the tawse slashed against her buttocks.

The hardest and most satisfying stroke yet.

Helen cried out. She violently shuddered against the pole, and what she felt was more than just an orgasm. As she climaxed, a sinewy sensation of equilibrium swept through her, encompassing her pain and her pleasure.

Sighing heavily, she pressed her hot forehead against the cold pole and slid her palms up and down the smooth metal, warm tears bathing her eyes.

Lyles gently ran the tips of his fingers across her stinging buttocks, his breath rough.

"Beautiful," he rasped. "So beautiful."

He pressed his long body along her back, his groin firmly cupping her tender ass. She felt his thick erection through the fabric of his slacks. He moved his mouth next to her ear.

"It was your employer. Not you."

"What?" Helen could barely speak. She was having another climax.

"I didn't choose your firm because of your employer. I didn't like him."

She managed a shaky laugh. "I don't like him either."

"Then resign. You're far too talented to work for the likes of him. Work for me instead. Design my house."

Helen nodded. She would have done anything he asked her to do. But to be asked to do something she loved required no prolonged consideration on her part.

Lyles slid his arms around her waist and held her against him, the warm softness of his slacks chafing the raw, tender skin of her ass.

"More?" he whispered.

She gripped the pole, arched her spine, and thrust her buttocks toward him. "Yes. More. Please."

Lyles moved away from her. The tawse whistled through the air. Helen threw back her head.

Pain.

Pleasure.

Equilibrium.

FIRST
TIME SINCE

Xan West

My dress boots rested in a neat line on the top of the book-case. And waited. It had been months since I wore anything but my work boots. Months since they were taken down to be cared for by a loving hand. Months since my slave asked to be released. They waited.

So did I. Waited for the gnawing feeling of failure to fade. Waited until I had thoroughly licked my wounds. Waited until it seemed possible to emerge from the safety of my cave and go out into the world again.

We build these intense relationships, fill them with ritual and intent and all of our full selves, and even if they end honor-ably (as this one did), that doesn't stop us from feeling ripped in two. Like a vital piece of self just walked out the door, never to return.

Rebuilding came first. Reclaiming all the tasks I delegated to him. All of the opportunities for service that I created led to this sense that we were one unit—interdependent. So I began to take them back. From the preparation of food, to putting away my clothes precisely as I require. From keeping my glass full to shaving my head every week.

But not my boots. They gathered dust as I tried to imagine feeling powerful enough, strong enough, whole enough to wear them. They were patient. More patient than I was with this grieving.

I slowly took over more and more tasks in my household. I reconnected with friends, not speaking of my grief but gaining warmth and strength from their touch and presence. I watched the bitterness of winter fade.

Newness in the air, I dragged myself to a leather conference I had agreed to teach at long before he asked for release. After unpacking, I sat alone in my hotel room and blacked my Frye boots for the first time in years. Slowly. With care. Tears fell on the leather as I sat in silence and brushed on the saddle soap, cleansing away four months of dust.

More than any other piece of gear, my boots are the core of my self as a dominant. They are an integral part of my play, a deep symbol of hierarchy. With my boot on the back of a man's neck, driving his face into the floor, there is complete clarity about who we are in relation to one another. Belly on the floor, abject before me, his mouth on my boots is a symbol of his reverence for my power. The sound of my boots on the floor reminds him of his place in my world. As the object of his worship, they are like bells in church, drawing his attention to the mystery of me.

With a dusky gleam on my feet, I stood in front of a large room, talking about kink I had not practiced in months, aware every second of the sensation of newly cared-for leather on my feet.

It was at this conference that I felt myself start coming back to life. I ached with new sensations, electric shocks of warmth moving through me. I felt my stride deepen in those boots, the sensation winding up my legs to my cock. I was conscious of it swelling as I moved through crowds, claiming space with the strength of my walk. I sat down in packed rooms, conscious of eyes on my boots, aware of the gaze of other men for the first time since.

I walked into the men's room and as I was unzipping in front of a urinal, I noticed a man kneeling on the floor, looking up at me, clad only in a chain collar with a large lock, and a yellow jock, waiting, a sign around his neck reading "urinal." His eyes were calm, as only one who has fully surrendered can be. I pulled out my cock and pissed on that calm face, watching the warmth run down his body as his eyes widened with joy at being used. I zipped up and then went to my room, where I removed my boots slowly and curled up on the bed, remembering the last time my former slave took my piss. I rocked, my arms wrapped round myself, knowing I had taken my first step back, and that was as much as I could handle right then.

A few months later, I went to the big party at a local leather weekend. Everybody dressed in their best gear. I went wearing no gear but my boots and a pair of denim shorts. I worked the volunteer shift I had committed to, the only thing that made me crawl out of my cave that night. And then I was free. I settled myself at a nest of couches and watched. I was greeted from time to time, but it was clear that I did not want to be approached. A man sat near me, in a chest harness, leather shorts, and lineman boots, with gorgeous large nipples. They called out to passersby, "Touch me" as they stood at attention. And many did. He was rarely alone for long. He would sit, an expression of serenity on his face. Within seconds, another man would approach him, greet him, and start working his nipples, sometimes grinding into his thighs or cock with boots, sometimes thrusting into his mouth with tongue or fingers, but always, always working those nipples, starting with fingers, stroking, then pinching, and soon moving on to teeth. He was floating in a sea of skin and hands, teeth and leather, and his expression did not change. He was rapt in prayer.

I watched him for a long time, my dick hardening. Then I walked over to the bootblack station. There was a boy working there I had been drawn to for awhile. Max was clearly too young for me, cocky (masking his uncertainty), self-centered, and rude to other submissives. Barely twenty-four, he was obviously not yet a man, perhaps not even interested in becoming one. Clearly in need of guidance and seeking intently. Someone I was utterly wrong for, and I knew it. I was not in a place where it even made sense to think of such a project.

Ever since my slave was released, Max kept appearing, whenever I emerged from my cave, offering himself. I was always sitting when he approached, sliding to his knees to speak to me, completely focused on me, sweetly recounting his escapades of late. I found it hard to keep my hands from rubbing his head as he spoke to me on those occasions. Touching him felt good, just right. Something would click into place as I put my hands on him. I knew he was not ready for me, and I definitely was not ready for him, but the draw was there. The last time I had seen him, just the night before, he had excitedly told me that he was bootblacking all weekend, a hopeful look on his face. As timing would have it, his chair was the only one free at the moment I arrived at the bootblack station. And so I sat, choosing to release some of this energy building between us in a controlled context.

His face lit up.

He was thoroughly pleased with himself, making conversation and fiddling with his tools. Then he started brushing on the saddle soap, the familiar smell drifting up to me. The sensation was so similar, and yet the energy was palpably different. This boy was intent on the job, focused and precise, and would pause, looking up at me, a sweet wide smile on his face. He always looked as if he had been caught in a moment of stillness between motions, just a pause before he would whirlwind around again. There was no serenity here, no contentment. Frenetic gladness, barely captured joy. That's what he embodied. His hands on my boots were electric, and I could feel myself jolted back to life, my dick throbbing as I pictured capturing this Puck-like being, holding him still and forcing him onto my cock, his body trembling with joy, filling us both with this electricity.

His head hovered near my thigh as he started to apply the polish, and my hand reached out to stroke it, and bring it to rest there, watching him closely to see if my touch was unwelcome. He sunk into it, murmuring, "Thank you, Sir. Thank you for this attention. I would be honored by any attention you have to offer, Sir."

I closed my eyes, feeling his hands on my boot and his breath against my cock. I could feel my boots springing to life as I casually stroked his face, my hand sliding against his lips. I breathed in slowly, feeling my dominance rising, a bittersweet sensation, and gripped my hand over his mouth, my eyes on his. His hands stilled on my boot, as I covered his airways, taking his breath. I watched that life surge, felt it against my palm, and held him, bringing him stillness. I released his breath and watched his eyes go starry as he found that lovely serene place. Then his hands resumed blacking my boot. I savored it, feeling myself surge, as I saw reverence fill him. He began to brush the boot, fumbling a bit, and dropped the brush a few times, apologizing softly. I pulled his chin up, meeting his eyes, my hand slowly stroking his cheek.

"Breathe, boy. I know you can do this."

He swallowed, trembling under my hand. He obeyed, taking a deep breath, letting it out slowly. His frame stilled, and his eyes darkened. He nodded once, firmly, and pulled his focus in. He began brushing my boots vigorously, heating and sealing the polish, a seriousness in his gaze as he brushed one and then the other. His hand steady, he used the rag to buff each of them.

He paused, and put his belly on the floor, looking up at me. And then he put his mouth on my boot. This was not in his regular blacking regimen; I knew that. We had discussed how he only licked the boots of those he would offer his submission to. I knew exactly what he was offering. I took it, for the first time since. I reached out and held a man's submission in my hand, savoring the feel of it.

I ground the sole of my boot into his back, using the heel to drive his mouth deeper into the leather, savoring the feel of a man on the floor under my boot. I could feel myself surging as his tongue stroked me, and I picked up and slammed my heel into his back, hearing his moan around my boot. I growled and rammed into his back, driving the heel in where I knew it was the sharpest, grabbing a yelp from him. I could see his hips thrusting into the floor, and I laid my boot heel on his lower back just above his ass, sliding the side of the boot into his crack as I wrapped his hair round my hand, pushing his mouth into my boot until I had his breath again. His ass shuddered under my boot and I watched him come, waiting to release his breath until it was over. His arms wrapped around my boot as he sobbed, and I stroked his hair lightly.

He stayed there for a few moments and then lifted his head to look up at me.

"May I please lick the other boot, Sir?" he asked.

"After you do something else for me. Am I your last client for the night?"

"Yes, my shift is over right now, Sir."

"Pack up your belongings and come with me."

"Yes, Sir."

He packed up his boot kit with trembling hands. He followed me to the dungeon, leaving the kit against the wall.

"Hands and knees."

"Yes, Sir."

He dropped instantly, and I immediately slammed my boot into him. I drove into him with rapid blows, ramming my boot into his thighs and ass.

"Move."

And I kicked him over to the horse. I paused, and ground my heel into his inner thigh watching his face contort with pain. I looked down at him, holding his eyes, and took in the sight of him under my boot, submission open on his face.

"Please, Sir. Please use me as you see fit."

And so I did, for the first time since. I unleashed my sadism into him, grinding my boot into his dick until tears filled his eyes, slamming my boots into his thighs, raining blows into his chest, a whirlwind of pain to hold him still. I bent him over the horse, ripping his clothes open to my fists and teeth, and did not pause until my cock was poised at his asshole, opening him. He was whimpering around the head, trying to take it in, straining for me. It was clear he had never taken someone of my girth, for all his slutting around, and he was struggling with it.

"Take it, boy."

"I don't know if I can, Sir." He was crying, his head shaking back and forth in frustration.

"Take it boy. I know you can take it for me."

"Yes, Sir," he whimpered.

I thrust home, forcing him open, making my way inside him. It was a joy to see his body trembling on my cock, feel his ass work to hold me. I went still inside him, watching him push himself to take it.

"That's it boy. Take my cock in your ass. Give yourself up to me."

I used him thoroughly that night, jamming my dick into him, mindless of anything but my own pleasure. As he sobbed, I fucked his tight ass, and reveled in my own control. I took his breath again as I came inside him, my cock bursting in what seemed like endless spurts.

I pulled out of his ass, and forced him to kneel on the floor and jack off onto my neglected boot, promising that he would have the opportunity to clean off his own spunk with his tongue. Tears streamed down his face, and after he came I ordered him to rub them into my boot, mix them in with the come.

"This is how you feed my boot, boy. With your come and your tears. Fill it up, and then lick it clean. That's it boy."

I kept my boot heel on the back of his neck as he licked the leather clean, feeling life surge through my body in delicious waves. I stroked him as he lay at my feet, softly praising his work. We stayed like that for a long time. Then I tucked a generous tip into his boots, patted him softly on the head, and walked out.

That night I slept well.

For the first time since.

OMEGA
TO ALPHA

Diana St. John

His online name was Ellis Dee.

Such audacity in naming appealed to my good-girl-wanna-be-bad nature. He came across as cool, confident, and, most importantly, dominant. Sweet Jesus, the rush of warmth and liquid lust that flowed through me, intoxicating me, as he described in detail just how he would spank me if I were there. I was amazed—I didn't even have to spill all of my fantasies. He had ideas of his own.

After a few evenings of online chat and a few phone calls, I found myself waiting for the college shuttle just outside the mailroom. I was wearing an autumn-toned little plaid skirt, baby-doll T-shirt, thigh highs and platforms, and feeling quite naughty, deliciously naughty, under the watchful eye of the nun in full habit who directed campus mail delivery.

The shuttle ride to the city bus stop seemed to take an eternity. The bus ride to a seedy apartment complex in Santa Monica was paradoxically fast. I wondered if my purpose was written all over my face. If the hairbrush and leather belt in my bag, my only toys at that point, were obvious to my fellow passengers. Could they tell by looking at me how long I had craved to feel them make impact, again and again, on my helpless, throbbing ass?

When I arrived at the apartment complex, I had a moment of concern for my safety. I hadn't told anyone where I was going, excited and aroused by the secrecy. I also knew that in my small Catholic women's college, it would be considered far more normal to get wasted and fucked by some nameless, faceless boy from the local public university's frat chapters than to be stone-cold sober and indulge in what I was beginning to realize was my spanking fetish.

I knocked on the door, heart racing. He answered and I'm sure there was some small talk, but I can't remember it. I only recall the current that raced from my stomach to my clit when he crooned in his lovely baritone voice, "So very naughty...skirt so short...brat..." He laughed, murmuring "Such a bad girl needing to be spanked" before guiding me over to the bed. He sat down on the edge and pulled me over his lap.

It was the moment I had been waiting for almost forever, heart pounding, holding my breath for the sound, the feel of skin on skin, the initial impact, and the lovely spread of warmth.

The bastard made me wait as he flipped up my skirt, pulled down the little pink excuse of a pair of panties that were already soaked, and began to rub my rump, telling me what a shame it was to have to punish such a lovely ass. I couldn't stop grinding into his thighs, surprising myself with the intensity of my desire. He merely laughed, loving how badly I wanted this. Finally, he began.

I heard the crack of a hand coming down on the sweet curve at the bottom of my right cheek and felt the sting melt into a

liquid heat that went from my ass to my cunt. Immediately, I
was hooked. Again and again his hand descended, and we both
realized at once that I was lifting my hips to meet his hand. He
began to murmur those utterly sexy threats about how I was
obviously hopelessly naughty, about me liking it too much. Then
he abruptly stopped. He told me to stand up and show him what
I had brought.

As I got to my feet, he flicked my clit and then commented
on how aroused I was. I was only aware that in my few experiences with lovers, I'd always needed additional lube, had never
been so wet that the juices were running down my thighs. I was
mortified—yet relieved—when I realized that I wasn't frigid, as
one of the nice boys from times past had hinted. I just needed
sex that was hot, hard, dirty, and nasty.

Pulling out my cocoa-colored leather belt and the white
plastic paddle-shaped hairbrush was almost harder than admit-
ting the spanking fetish itself. I fantasized about being spanked
every morning as I brushed my long dark brown hair, but this
was different. This was real. The wide smile that crossed his face
as I tentatively handed over my treasures assuaged my tension,
and his instantaneous reaction of pulling me back over his lap
could only have been more perfect had he grabbed me by my
hair to put me back in my place.

The hairbrush.

Mother of God, the hairbrush!

It had a more resounding quality, a bit more thud and sting
than his hand. My writhing in lust was joined by that instinctive
desire to cover, and the absolute reality that I was nowhere near
wanting to use my safeword. If he had stopped, I would have
been as frustrated as if he had denied me an orgasm. He seemed
to anticipate my hand's movement, had waited for it, I'm sure,
and pinned my hand at the small of my back, promising in that

sexy growl to tie me to the bedframe and use the belt if I tried that again.

Such a sweet threat to a brat's ears...

It's good when a top keeps a promise delivered in the heat of lust. More to test his resolve (would he take me where I needed to go?) and less because I wanted to shield my red, burning ass, I wrestled my hand free as if to cover my butt, and he laughed again before delivering a long series of stinging swats to my thighs. The last one cracked the plastic hairbrush and made us both laugh in surprise.

But he kept his promise. He pulled me to my feet, stood up, and arranged some pillows on the bed to prop up my hips. Then he pushed me back down and used scarves to tie me. He pulled my wrists overhead and tied them to the headboard. He spread my legs, tying each ankle to a corner of the bed. Even with my baby doll T-shirt and skirt still on, I felt exposed in a way I'd never experienced even while totally naked. He flipped my skirt back up and picked up the belt, pressing the cool leather against my hot, red ass, tracing it lightly against the skin, teasing my inner thighs and startling the hell out of me when the first lick landed squarely on my clit rather than my ass. The sound that escaped me, a low moan of raw lust, revealed my desire to keep this going.

My desire for more and more.

The feel of leather on my body was a skin-to-skin contact of the most primal kind. He alternated cheeks, then thighs, then careful blows directly on my dripping wet cunt that I thought might make me climax if he continued long enough. But he didn't. He went back to laying the strokes evenly across my ass. He taught me the dance of this form of desire and pushed me to what I thought might be a limit of sensation. The fiery heat on my bottom became nearly unbearable before he backed off, rubbing, pinching, teasing my clit, and repeating, stretching my limits and leaving me wanting even more.

Finally, when he decided I'd had enough, he introduced me to another deep form of pleasure. He dropped the belt, and the buckle made a satisfying clink as it hit the floor. He stepped into my field of vision, unzipped his jeans, and pulled out his cock. The last shred of doubt, the tiniest bit of fear that he would think my desires odd was put to rest when I realized he was gloriously aroused.

There was no resistance as he plunged his cock into my slick pussy and began fucking me hard. His hips pounded against my throbbing ass as he reached around and teased my clit with his fingers. The climax that had been building from the first moment his hand landed on my skin burst forth in waves radiating out from my ass and pussy. My orgasm consumed my whole body with an intensity I had never experienced before. The walls of my pussy gripped his cock with the rhythm of my climax. With a few more deep thrusts, he came.

The pleasantries we exchanged afterwards were as easily forgotten as those beforehand. What was more memorable was the realization that there was no turning back, no forgetting the throbbing heat of my ass or the mind-blowing climax I'd just had. The pleasure of pain was just too good.

CROSSED

Rachel Kramer Bussel

I'm strung up on a St. Andrew's cross, blindfolded, my breasts pressing through the space of the X as I face the wall, my back and ass exposed to any and all who want to look. And though my eyes may be covered, there are plenty who want to look. I can hear them chattering behind me while my husband, Chuck, readies his implements. I'm nervous, but the kind of nervous that makes my pussy tighten, my nipples harden. I like being nervous, I like trying new things. I like being pushed to my limits.

There's a leather ball gag shoved in my mouth. I happen to know it's purple, but only because Chuck told me after he'd blindfolded me. He bought it especially for me—large. I know because he used to use a smaller one on his ex, but he told me I not only have a bigger mouth, but I'm a bigger brat, and I needed more of a challenge. I'm such a competitive, horny slut that hearing this only made me open wide as could be. We both have mixed feelings about gags—at the right time, there is nothing hotter than hearing a man or woman scream in ecstasy as she gets beaten in all the right ways. Those piercing cries can fill a room and become the perfect soundtrack to sadism. But there is also a charm in watching someone struggle, in being aware that those screams exist, but for the moment are locked away, known only to the one holding them in. It's like watching a silent movie, and the noise has to transform into some other outlet of pain, be it a wrenched face or muscle spasms or twisting and writhing, all of which can send any true sadist into orbit.

I should know, because despite my current enjoyable predicament, I am one—a sadist, I mean. See, the two of us are switches, meaning that we go both ways kinkwise. We can get off on being held down, controlled, dominated, as well as being the one inflicting the best kind of pain in the world. I have been known to grin as widely as a lottery winner when I've got him over my knee and turn his wide ass a beautiful shade of rose. But I can't deny that being strung up, immobilized, cuffed into place is also one of the most highly charged fantasies I have.

We like to spice things up to make sure our lives never get stagnant. So for the annual BDSM conference we attend in our nation's capital, far from our small Iowa town, we decided to bet on who would be the top and who would be the bottom for this momentous occasion, and who could get the other off the fastest. Having been high school sweethearts and marrying at age 20 (we're now 42), we know a lot about how to make each other come. But apparently he knew just that much more than me, clocking in at three minutes, six seconds, while it took me three minutes, twenty-two seconds to make Chuck come in my mouth. Not that I'm complaining—first because I love blowing him and would gladly linger on his cock for an hour; and second because now here I am, with a whole audience watching my still trim ass and strong back as I await what will happen next.

Once the bet was decided, we didn't talk about the details.

We have our fair share of kinky implements, but they're the kind that can be easily put away when company comes. We don't have any fancy equipment, which makes events like this a special treat for us, ones we fantasize about alone and together. We only attend about one a year, but when we're there, we make the most of every minute of playtime. We're often the first ones in the dungeon and sometimes the last to leave. So while it wasn't an entirely unknown setting, the precise mechanics of what would take place were left a mystery, to me anyway. While we might talk about what other couples we wanted to invite back to our hotel room or which workshops we'd attend, the actual details about what would happen while I was strung up had been kept secret.

So there I am, my arms above my head, fastened in securely with padded black leather cuffs. My ankles are similarly bound. Just as I mentally wish for some stimulation of my nipples, Chuck reaches around me and pinches each of them. I can't see, but I don't need to in order to know he's twisting them in this way he has that hurts and arouses me in equal measure. "Kathy," he breathes in my ear. "Are you going to be a good slut for me? The perfect little pain slut?"

"Yes, Sir," I tell him, deferring to the honorific I use when I bottom to him (he calls me "Mistress" when I top him). My reward is a set of vibrating nipple clamps that he attaches to each protruding bud, making me whimper. I'm glad that I'm facing the wall as opposed to a whole group of people, though that would bring its own sort of humiliation if they could all see me get my breasts whipped without me seeing them. As it is, I'm sure my cheeks are blushing, and the other set will be soon as well.

"What do you think of her ass?" I hear him ask the audience.

"Spank it!"

"Fuck it!"

"Hot—I want a piece of that," I hear. If anyone in our hometown could see me now, they'd be either shocked and embarrassed or laughing hysterically, because they know me as the simple, plain woman who runs the local drugstore, always ready with a smile and medication. I know almost everyone there, but they don't really know me. Not the real me, this me. These virtual strangers I see only once a year get to witness the true Kathy, the one who comes out on rare occasions but is hungry for everything kink can offer.

Being bound like this allows me to let go in ways I couldn't otherwise. I love pain, as Chuck has correctly stated, but I need to be held in place in order to enjoy it to the utmost. Like this, I'm not my job or my family or even from Iowa. All I am is a pain slut, a girl who likes to be tied up, a girl who's offering up her ass for whatever may come next.

"Would you like to do the honors?" I hear Chuck ask.

I shiver, my bonds keeping me in place as I feel moisture start to drop from my wide-open pussy. What will he be doing while they torment me?

I don't have long to wonder as I bite my lip and feel a searing blow land evenly across both my buttcheeks. I whimper, and then feel soft hair brush against my inner thigh before someone is shoving what I think is a dildo into my wetness. The toy goes easily all the way inside me as another strike lands across my ass. My teeth sink deeper into my lip, not enough to draw blood but enough to make marks as the combination of getting fucked and spanked takes over.

"Oh yeah," a deep Southern voice drawls as whoever is fucking me starts really pounding the dildo into me. And then I learn what exactly my husband's role is when our familiar flogger falls sharply against my upper back. He knows that my back is right up there with my cunt and my nipples as an erogenous zone. I like to get bitten there, bitten to the point that he leaves marks, bitten until I scream. I like backrubs where the masseuse's hands seem to become part of my skin, entering me on one side and leaving on the other. I like to get turned inside out, and Chuck knows this all too well. I have no escape route as the thuds of the flogger reverberate through my body.

Don't get me wrong—it's not that I want one. I like being the kind of woman who goes places other women don't. I like being someone who goes right up to the edge of what she can stand, and sometimes beyond that. But sometimes I scare myself, just a little, emitting the kind of gasp you give in a haunted house, where you know you're an adult, an intelligent, aware, self-reliant adult, and yet you can manage to spook yourself enough to make this sound.

That's what it feels like, in a way. It isn't quite the same as being suspended, where every ripple of the rope threatens to send you to the ground, where every motion rocks you to and fro. Here there is only solid wood and me, and my body is absorbing every shock. I'm getting fucked and flogged at the same time, my entire back, ass, pussy, legs open to whoever wants to look.

Part of me loves that. I'm a shameless slut and, in theory, each audience member could take turns coming up here and shoving something inside me, or running their hands all over me. Secretly, I sometimes fantasize about being bound, gagged, and blindfolded while strangers tease me, never letting me get off, only stroking or pinching or slapping or stinging for brief moments, enough to make me moan but not to come.

But there's another part of me that, in the middle of a public scene, freezes up. I tense, sure that some long-lost schoolteacher or friend of my parents will recognize my naked body and run to blab it to our hometown paper. I become convinced that someone, somewhere, will suddenly realize that I'm not the nice girl I pretend to be but rather this other girl, one who, in the grip of lust, will display herself for anyone who wants to watch. Or touch. Because the truth is, the person shoving the giant dildo inside me, the person who is about to make me come, could be anyone. He could be a hot young stud with a giant cock, someone I'd gladly spread my legs for, or he could be someone embodying everything I can't stand—too much facial hair, smoker's breath, chauvinist tendencies. He could even be a Republican for all I know.

And that's the beauty and the danger of an event like this. We're all here together, for one common purpose, and we all get reduced to that lowest common denominator where all social graces get stripped away. Being unable to escape physically thanks to my bonds is nothing compared to knowing how open I've left myself in other ways. I'm not only trusting my husband, who is wielding his flogger with increasingly sadistic delight, but myself. I'm trusting that I won't collapse, break down, come unglued. Or maybe I'm trusting that I will do all those things, that I will walk away from this event a changed woman.

Maybe you're wondering how all those thoughts can coalesce in my mind while I'm bound to the cross getting flogged and fucked with a dildo. If so, you don't quite get me yet, and that's okay. I'm hyperactive, type A squared, my mind constantly flying from one thought to the next. Sensation has to be extreme before I yield to it. Thankfully, Chuck knows this. The dildo stops, and soon I feel fingers approaching me there, between my wide open legs. They are gentler, and softer, and I know they are female. Chuck stops flogging me, and I'm pretty sure it's because he wants to watch. He loosens the gag, pulling it down so it's around my neck. Now that I'm free to scream, I have no desire to. I'd rather get praised for being strong enough to take it.

Chuck's fingers grab my hair and pull me back while mystery woman's lubed-up hand starts entering me. "How much do you want?" he asks me.

I have no idea at first what he's trying to get at. "The whole thing?" I ask, because I'm not sure. There is an unbelievable pressure in my cunt, a small hand, a fist, rocking against me. I've taken a fist before but never in this position.

"That's a given," he says, releasing my head and pushing it forward. My head is pretty much the only part of me not strapped down to a piece of wood, yet my mouth, from here, is pretty much useless. I long to suck my husband off, but now is not the time.

"How does she feel, Gaia?" Chuck asks.

"She's tight, but I think she could take even more," I hear the woman say.

Then I do moan, not caring anymore about being stoic. It feels like she's going to rip me in two, and then I also never want her to leave. She pulls out and adds more lube, and then slides back inside. The tension, that sweet, special tension, eases up just a little.

"Then give it to her," Chuck says. I know if I could see, he'd be giving me a look telling me not to argue. So I don't. And finally, all those messy, swirling thoughts give way, at least for the moment, as this Gaia woman slides her other hand up inside me. Where it goes I'm not sure, but I know it's there. At first, my instinct is to tighten up even more, but then I let go. I try to spread my legs, though I know that's pointless. I experiment with every way I can think of to ease the pressure, and only when I totally sink into the warmth and heat and fullness of her hands do I appreciate the gift my husband has given me.

There is a completely different energy in the room now. Instead of wondering what the others think, I feel at one with them. We are all getting double-fisted together, fucked in holes we never knew we had, in ways we couldn't have conceived of. We are all in this together, and when I come, practically pushing her hands out of me, the room stirs, the air around me chilling my already cool skin. My orgasm is like a flame setting a wick on fire, rising from my toes to my head, blue to orange to black smoke. When she exits, it's like I've given birth to her.

The room is quiet, and it's not until the blindfold comes off that I realize I'm crying. Not crying, really, but tears are there, seeping out of me. Chuck folds me into a blanket and whisks me back to our room. He's probably arranged for some pretty sub to clean up after us in the hope of a spanking later.

Losing the bet taught me so many lessons, but one of the greatest was that when it comes to kink, it's not a matter of who comes the fastest but who comes the hardest. And in that I had certainly won.

MY
MAINSTREAM
GIRLFRIEND

Stephen Elliott

L isten. I always thought I was kinky. I've always read bondage porn and jerked off to videos of women wrestling or stories of teachers blackmailed into sexual servitude by their students. I used to stand in the bookstore rereading Eric Stanton comics until I finally saved the eighty dollars to buy the Taschen coffee-table book. But yesterday my girlfriend came over and something happened that made me think I might not be kinky anymore. She was wearing ruby slippers, like Dorothy in *The Wizard of Oz*. But she was also wearing torn fishnets with a garter belt, sexy underwear, a long black dress over a lacy slip. A lot of women would feel self-conscious dressed so sexy, but I have an awesome girlfriend.

We do a lot of stuff that some people might think is outside the mainstream. Like, we'll go to a party and she'll sit on the couch and point to the floor and I'll sit on the floor in front of her. It's a power thing. There'll be colleagues from the university I teach at, other writers. Some of my friends think it's weird. But it's not really that weird. Also, sometimes she'll put a collar on my neck and I'll wear it around the house. I talked to my roommates about it. I told them to keep in mind that I clean the bathroom when she comes over, so if they want a clean bathroom they have to be OK with the other stuff.

Often she'll spank me really hard, or hit me with a whip. If she wants me to be emotionally vulnerable she'll kick me out of the bed and make me sleep on the floor for a while. It doesn't take long before I start to break. I'm not an emotionally strong person. A lot of times when she ties me up and she's hurting me, smacking my balls or my face or pulling really hard on my nipples, I'll start to cry. I'll think about my father or some of the things that happened when I was a kid. It's called trauma play: I eroticize my childhood abuse.

One time I cried when she had her hand in my ass. We had only just started dating. I was lying on a towel on my back and she was looking at me, watching me closely. She was wearing a latex glove and using a lot of lube. She slid one finger in, then another. I felt her reach inside me, curl her fingers. I started to panic. I told her it hurt. It burned. It always hurt but it was just two fingers. How much could a finger hurt? I told her I was worried. I confessed I was worried that I was dirty, that there would be shit on her finger. I didn't even know it until I said it but the truth rolled across me like a plow. Then I told her I was more worried about that than anything in the world and I started crying and I cried for a long time. I thought, Man, I am so fucked up.

"I'm sorry," was all I could say. "Please don't leave."

She kept her hand inside me, stroking my hair with her other hand. "Look at me," she said. She was leaning in close to me and I could see that she loved me on every line in her face. "I think you're amazing," she said, and I cried some more.

But now I don't feel so self-conscious about my ass. Freud take note, maybe my girlfriend has taken me out of the anal stage? Recently she's been fucking me with a strap-on. Which is what she did yesterday.

I've been fucked with a strap-on before. Often a really small one or just very briefly. Normally I start screaming right away: "It hurts! It hurts! It hurts!" That hasn't always stopped the other person.

The first time I really open up to her she has me tied to the table in the middle of my room. She's good with knots, and she has lots of rope. Admittedly, being tied to a table and ass-fucked is pretty kinky. And it was only a week ago. And my whole point here is that maybe I'm not that kinky anymore, but I'm getting to that. I'm not there yet. Stay with me. So she's fucking me. She goes in really slow, whispering me through it. "There's no hurry," she says. And for the first time it really doesn't hurt. I can feel her going in and out of me and it just feels good. The cock is probably seven or eight inches long and average width. I can feel my asshole stretched around it. She's picking up speed. I get this whole euphoric feeling. Like I'm on ecstasy or something. It washes across me. I feel so good. I feel great. I'm in love with everybody, and with my girlfriend in particular. My arms are pulled forward, nipple clamps run from my nipples to my wrists. The clamps pull on my nipples every time she slams into my ass. And I start talking all dirty. I'm like, "Oh, yeah. Please. Fuck. Me. Fuck me. Fuck me." Like I'm in a porno or something. But it feels good to say. And she likes it.

I couldn't believe it didn't hurt.

So what happened yesterday is that my girlfriend came over dressed all sexy. There's nothing kinky, I think, about admiring a woman who is dressed sexy. And she's great looking all the time anyway. I mean, my girlfriend is super-hot. I'm not saying she's not really smart, interesting, political, compelling, or caring. She is. But that's not what I'm talking about here. What I'm trying to say is that my girlfriend has the kind of body that could stop a train. I'm lucky. She likes me. What am I supposed to do about that? Talk her out of it? No way.

So she came over and she wanted to fuck me. She's leaving for two weeks to rebuild a Buddhist temple in Mississippi and she wanted to have sex before she left and by sex she meant she wanted to fuck my ass. I hadn't known she was coming over and there was still a small piece of rope on the floor from the last time she tied me to the table and the table was still in the center of the room. I apologized for that and she hit me a couple of times with the rope. Then I went down on her.

Then she spread a towel on my bed and lubed up my ass. We use Liquid Silk. Elbo Grease lasts longer but Liquid Silk seems to work better. At least that's been our experience together. Maybe different lubes work differently on different assholes. Hard to say.

She takes off her dress and her slip rises and falls across her knees. She takes that off and it's just her beautiful vintage underwear, the naked tops of her thighs and her torn fishnets with the ivory garter and ruby slippers. I watch her put the harness on, sliding the black silicone cock into its binding, pulling the rubber over the head. "OK," she says. "Ass up in the air."

She's fucking me again. She told me before that every guy wants something in his ass. She's a sex worker so she would know. Apparently it's the big secret among men, the thing men don't talk about with each other. I brought it up earlier in the week with my friend Josh. Josh is a science writer and I was staying at his house in Los Angeles for a couple of days. There was a party I was down there for. I shook Bill Maher's hand. That's another story. But the point is I mentioned this to Josh, that my girlfriend had told me every guy wants something in his ass. He explained that there were all these nerve endings and that the prostate was like a male G-spot. He was dropping me off at the Burbank airport and I got the impression, though he didn't come right out and say it, that he enjoyed having things in his ass, too. So I figure my girlfriend is right. She usually is. So you see what I'm saying? Nothing so kinky about what we're doing here. She's fucking me in the ass and it feels really good but then every guy wants something in his ass.

I look back at her. She's still wearing her ruby slippers with their little heels. She has one knee down and the other knee up, like she's being knighted. Her left foot is planted firmly on the bed to give her leverage and she's gripping me by the hips, pulling me back into her. All I can see are her shoes and her legs in her fishnets. I wish I had a picture of it. On my end I'm just trying to keep the rhythm. I can't help but let out all these little moans of pleasure. I'm having a really good time. Here's what makes me think I'm not kinky anymore. This time, instead of thinking about my father and all the bad stuff that happened when I was younger, I'm thinking about what she looks like fucking me. I'm also thinking about a hamburger and a chocolate shake. I'm being fucked and it feels really good and I'm thinking, Oh man, I would *love* a chocolate shake right now. It's a deep hunger, a deep sex hunger. That's not just normal, that's all-American.

After she fucks me for a while and I get that my-girlfriend-fucked-the-hell-out-of-me glow, I go down on her some more. She slips her underwear off and puts her dress back on and then hikes it up, lowering her ass onto my face. I'm surrounded by her magnificent ass. With her dress over me her pussy and ass are my entire world. I'm eating her out, her legs pinning my arms. I'm ravenous for her. I love the way she tastes. I didn't used to like the way a woman tastes but my girlfriend cured me of that. I want to get my tongue deep inside of her. I want to lick her heart. I go down on her for so long that the next day my neck hurts.

So there it is. I thought I was so kinky, so alternative. But really I'm just a guy who appreciates sexy clothes, likes something in his ass, and loves going down on his girlfriend. After sex I like a big meal. Normal.

There was one thing. Since she was leaving for a while she carved POSSESSION in my side with the knife she keeps by my bed. She says she needs to sharpen it. She's been using it too much and it's getting dull. But she wanted me to be able to look in the mirror and think of her while she's gone. Also, in case I met another woman, that other woman would know there was already someone in my life when she saw POSSESSION recently cut into my skin. It's like those stickers on aspirin bottles that let you know this product was packaged for Walgreens and if you're buying it anywhere else you're taking part in some sort of crime. Labeling. I admit it, a lot of people aren't comfortable with cutting. Cutting is still "kinky." I have all these marks all over me from where she's cut me. But really, it's a small thing. I spend much more time with my face between her legs than I do getting cut. You have to look at the percentages. More and more I feel like I'm joining mainstream America.

ROCK PAPER SCISSORS

Shanna Germain

Rock, paper, scissors. That's what I've always called it.

Shim-sham-bo. His name for the game. Maybe he made it up, maybe he didn't.

Whatever we call it, it's how we play.

"Shim," he says, and our closed fists slap into our open palms. I watch his hands. Not because they might help me win but because I like to watch his hands. I know where they've been, where they will be. I know the short nails, cut to the quick for Sunday mornings on the guitar. I know the blue veins that pulse from arm to wrist to fingers, the half-moon scar that outlines his knuckle.

"Sham." The ring he always wears—wide silver circle on his ring finger—flashes when he brings his fist down. Beneath that band of silver, the word that I know is traced into his flesh. Red ink. Blood ink. A name. Mine.

"Bo," he says.

Our hands go out at the same time. I throw paper first. I always do. So does he. You can look it up online, what it says about your personality if you throw paper more than rock or scissors. Quietly powerful. Strongly submissive. Topping from the bottom.

We keep our hands out, flat hands with the palms down. He has the best hands. Spanking hands. But it's a tie. We play best out of three, and ties don't count.

"Again," he says.

"Shim-sham-bo," he says, faster, and he throws a rock. The fist. Loose enough that it could unfurl into something else. Tight enough that it is all power.

I throw paper again. I'm sending mixed signals. My hand in the spanking form, when really, it's his hand that I want, spanking.

"Your win," he says, sliding his rock hand under my paper hand. Paper covers rock. Curve of ass beneath flat of palm.

"Damn," I say. Neither of us wants to win this game. I'm a sub. So is he. Two subs in a relationship. This game is how we make it work. Loser takes all. Winner is the one who must wield the power. We could alternate, I guess, be fair. But that's not our style. It's not nearly as much fun.

"Go," he says, impatient. I grin and flash my eyes to the crotch of his jeans. Already the wide outline of his cock is visible through the fabric. I want to rub myself up against it like a cat, sniff it like a dog.

"Rock," I say. Our fists make small noises against our palms. I inhale the sound, imagine it's his hand against my skin instead of his own.

"Paper." Somewhere, in my mind, I am already bent over, beneath his hand. I am already feeling the slide of my panties down my ass, across my thighs. In my mind, the small calluses in his palm scrape my skin...

"Scissors," I say.

And that's what he throws. Two fingers out, two fingers that will enter me if I can find a way to lose. Two fingers that will tweak my nipples. That will slap my clit with the same precision with which he slaps his guitar. The thump of rhythm. The heat-strum.

Me, I fall back on paper. I can see by his eyes that he didn't expect it. Three anythings in a row is risky, paper especially so. Chances are good I won't throw it again—it's human nature to mix things up, to tweak a pattern if we can. I've just given him an advantage. Maybe.

"Your win," I say.

"Fuck." He shakes his hands out, cracks his knuckles. That sound alone sends small shivers through me. He always pops his knuckles before he spanks me. He likes to make me wait, bent over at his feet, while he cracks each finger, so slowly I can feel the snap inside my body. So slowly that I count as he goes. *One, two...*it takes him forever to get to ten.

"Shim," he says. I watch his hands. Because I like to watch his hands, but also now because it might help me win. Lose. People think this is a game of chance, but no. How badly do I want to win? How badly does he? What is our fallback throw? He throws rock when he's confident. Scissors when he's nervous.

"Sham." His half-moon scar shines white. The ring flashes its promise of cool pressure against my skin. Beneath it, the top of a word written in red ink slides in and out of view. He clears his throat, and suddenly, I know what to throw.

"Bo," he says, and his scar and ring and scissors flash.

My hand, my winning-losing throw of paper, settles into the current of air and hangs between us.

"Bend over," he says. Now he is all rock.

I fold like paper, waiting for his hand. Red ink on white skin, marking me, slicing me open, once again.

ALL IN
THE WRIST

Alison Tyler

You throw like a girl," Elijah said, sneering from over his bottle of beer.

"I *am* a girl."

"But you don't have to throw like one."

I turned my head to give him my best fuck-you glare, which he ignored, his dark blue eyes focused instead on the way I stood facing the dartboard. He didn't seem impressed. One last swallow from the dark green bottle, and then he slid off the leather bar stool and came to stand behind me. His arms snuck around my waist as if to embrace rather than to instruct. "See? Like this," positioning my hand, pulling my elbow back. I shut my eyes as I felt his strong body against mine.

We hadn't slept together yet.

For six long months, we'd been engaged in that push-me pull-you dance. His teasing, flirtatious glances kept me up at night as I replayed each moment of our meetings. Double-entendres drenched every conversation. I always felt off-balance in his presence, as if I couldn't get proper footing. Now here he was, taking charge yet again.

"Some people aim from the ear," he explained, "but I like to line the shot up from the nose." His hand on my arm felt warm as he adjusted my stance. A tremor ran through me. "Now pull your arm back and throw."

How could I? Not when his cock was pressed against my ass like that—why had I worn a dress this thin? Why had fuchsia G-string panties seemed like a good idea? Elijah's chest pressed firmly into my back. I thought of the way he looked in his once-black jeans and crimson Sex Pistols T-shirt.

Forget *God Save the Queen.*

Who was going to save me?

When I opened my eyes, I caught our reflection in the window next to the dartboard: he looked like someone who knew how to play darts. But he also looked like someone who might steal your wallet if you left the bag open by his side. What had Trish said about him when he'd first walked through the door to our office?

"Hold onto your panties, honey. This boy's trouble."

I'd been typing a letter, focused on telling the little MacWindow icon to go fuck itself, and hadn't turned to look at Elijah until he had draped himself over the counter in front of my desk, package for my boss in his hand, leather wrist cuffs right at my eye level.

The sight of those cuffs had made me wet, and I'd turned into a stuttering fool as I'd signed for the package, trying not to stare at the pounded leather yet wondering what the cuffs would feel like tight around my own wrists.

"Come on," Elijah insisted now, words low in my ear. "You'll hit the bull's-eye if you shoot like I explained."

I took a deep breath and felt a shudder work through me.

"Move away," I told him. "Let me have a little room."

I could hear the smile in his voice. "See? The proper positioning has given you attitude you didn't have before." He didn't move, though. I could still feel his heat, bleeding through his clothes to me. "Now, remember. It's all in the wrist."

"So you said," I snapped, feeling the way my body wanted to mold to his. The way I could have set the dart down, spun around, and let him lift me up, so that my legs would part automatically around his flat waist. I could see the position easily: His hands cradling my ass, holding me steady. But my submission was what he wanted, wasn't it? That's what he expected.

"Step back, Elijah," I insisted. "I can't throw when you're breathing down my neck." My competitive nature refused to allow me to buckle. I couldn't let him win so easily.

"Like this?" his breath silky on my skin. Then his lips, pressed soft at the curve of my shoulder. Why had I worn a sundress on this date? I should have put on jeans and a turtleneck, covering up from neck to ankle. I'd seen the way he'd looked at me each time he dropped off a package, knew the way my body responded to those sultry glances.

"He's into leather," Trish had said, stating the obvious. "Did you see those cuffs?"

I'd swallowed hard and tried to act nonchalant, but all I'd been able to think of were the cuffs on his wrists, cuffs he might put on my wrists, snapped together, attaching the two.

"And you know what boys into leather are like."

"What are they like?" I'd asked, staring at Elijah through the window to the street. Watching him straddle his bike.

"Kinky little fuckers," Trish said smugly. "You can see what he wants to do to you. It's all in the eyes."

I hadn't wanted to tell her she was wrong. It was all in the wrists. Once securely cuffed, I'd be his, wouldn't I? His to do with whatever he desired.

Not yet, I reminded myself now. Make him work a little harder. Don't be as easy as a signature on a piece of paper. I elbowed back against him, and, laughing, he finally stepped away.

This wasn't my first time at a dartboard. Usually when I throw, I connect. Somewhere round the edge, sure, but definitely on the felt. I'm not pathetic by any means, but bull's-eyes are rare. This time, with his eyes on me, I would have loved to have hit that board dead center. When my dart landed in the wall outside of the ring, I felt my cheeks go scarlet.

The laughing behind me continued.

"You make me nervous," I said out the side of my mouth. "The way you're watching me."

"How am I watching you?"

I turned my head to gaze at him. "Like you want to fuck me."

As soon as I said the words, I realized I had everything wrong. Because his eyes became an even darker shade of blue, and he pulled in his lower lip, catching it between his sharp teeth. Suddenly, from that look alone, I understood.

You hear about time stopping. You hear about the crowds disappearing, about the world coming to a standstill. But not this evening. The bar was still there. The customers milling around us were still talking. Pool cues clicked. Foam frothed over glass mugs.

And yet there was only him and me.

He held my gaze, as if with his fists instead of his eyes. I could sense the hunger in him, and I realized that I'd become sure-footed, nimble even in my glossy high heels. My smile was the first real one I'd felt that night, one that was natural. In a heartbeat, I was glad for my dress, thin to the point of near-transparency yet no longer feeling flimsy. You had to be bold to wear a dress like this in a dive bar. That's what I suddenly was. Bold.

"I got that wrong, didn't I?" I asked, not bothering to lower my voice. His flippancy seemed to have vanished. He didn't respond. "*I'm* the one who's going to fuck you, aren't I?"

I didn't wait for his yes. I didn't need to hear the word. The game was on. I turned away from him, found the proper position, stood my ground, threw the dart. If I hadn't made the shot, where would we have been? I don't know. I don't have to worry about that. The dart flew clear and swift, hitting dead center as if to seal the deal.

Bull's-eye.

We were out of the bar in fast motion. No words. No need for them. To my place, down the street and up the steps. Three quick flights side by side. He seemed to have grown thinner, sleeker, a black cat at night. Into the apartment in a rush, no time even to put on the fan. The heat seemed to part for us. We were drawn forward, down the hall to my bedroom through the wet, sticky air. I didn't have to tell him to strip.

How had I missed the signs during all of those flirting conversations? How had I not seen the truth? He didn't want to fuck me. He didn't want to be on top. Elijah didn't want to cuff me to the bed.

I pictured the way he'd looked when I'd said the words aloud. I saw that glint in his eye, the nervous tug of his teeth on his lip. The knowledge changed me, like his hand on my arm had. Positioning me. Giving me the power to do what I wanted.

"On the bed," I told him once he was naked, my voice sounding so very much like the way he had told me how to throw that dart. "Hands over your head."

He obeyed without a word while I took in his lean body. The tattoos on his shoulders, twisted colorful images I'd never seen before, ones previously hidden by his ever-changing parade of concert T-shirts. His chest, ribs, hard flat belly. Sterling silver rings adorning both of his nipples. Another vibrant tattoo winding down toward his groin.

I had dressed like a princess, like a present to be unwrapped, when all along he was the one who needed undoing. He was the one who wanted my power. Fuck it all, the boy was stunning. Why hadn't I known he was sub?

His belt pulled easily from the loops of his jeans. In seconds, his body was held in place, wrist cuffs linked together and then looped through and attached to my bedframe by his own leather belt. I watched him swallow hard. I could hear the sneer still in my head, his voice plucking at me: "You throw like a girl." Then I gazed at the mirror over my 1940s vanity and saw the way I looked now.

A girl. Yes. I was a girl. But a different kind of girl. The kind of girl who could make Elijah's dreams come true. The kind of girl who could give a boy some pain if that's what he needed, if hurt was what made him fly.

Transformations can happen in the strangest places. Don't fairy tales teach us this when we're young? Magic is all around us. If you look hard enough. If you say the right words and click your ruby heels three times. If you know how to pull back your arm and release the weapon, the dart flies swift and true every time.

"On your stomach," I said, and he rolled over without a word of protest. I saw the rest of the tattoos now, the way the art made his bare skin more naked looking. The pale parts so vulnerable, the colors so alive.

He'd lost the game at the bar, but that didn't mean he wasn't going to win.

For six months we'd bantered, each time he'd come into the office. Dropping off packages, a courier with an attitude, never even glancing at the blonde buxom Trish, eyes only on me. I'd grown to look forward to his visits, began dressing better in anticipation of his 4 p.m. arrival. How had I missed the signs?

I found what I needed in my closet, a belt with silver studs, something hard, something fierce. The studs felt cold when I ran my thumb over the raised design. The tremor that worked through me now came from me imagining what this belt would feel like if I were the one tied to the bed. I pressed the leather against his skin, saw him grow still. Felt him waiting. The pressure between us was palpable. I could have traced the electricity in the air with my fingertip.

I looked down at the belt in my hands, imagined that dart in my right, and the feeling of shooting to the bull's-eye filled me once more. Then I doubled the leather and let the belt slap against his ass. Once. Hard. He sucked in his breath but didn't say a word. Did I hit like a girl? Was he thinking that? I knew I wasn't. I was whipping him like a dom. Slashing into his skin with a ferocity that couldn't be associated with male or female, but with sex in general.

The studs on the belt caught his skin and he groaned, but he didn't protest. The cool silver metal must have hurt like hell, but his body told me to continue. Again I snapped the leather. Again. His hips beat a silent rhythm against my mattress. He wanted what I had to give. That's what his looks had told me all this time. I simply hadn't known this was something I could offer. Hadn't looked into myself to see what he had seen.

Magic—what one person can do to another.

My panties grew wetter as I worked him. I could breathe in the slippery scent of my own arousal, growing brighter with each line that bloomed on his skin. He sucked in his breath as I pulled back my arm, as I struck him evenly, neatly across his ass.

What was he thinking, I wondered, watching his hips twitch. Was he remembering our previous conversations? That sexy banter we shared near the end of each day? Was he thinking of how I looked when he watched me through the plate glass windows, seeing me watch him get back on his bike and disappear once more into frantic San Francisco traffic?

The leather made a lovely sound when the belt connected. A sound like applause, a sound I'd been waiting my whole life to hear.

Had he known from the start that a night with me would end up like this?

I let the belt catch him hard, and the music of his dark hollow moan made me clench my thighs together. I could come from this, I thought. I could come.

And so could he. I dropped the belt, put my hand on his hot skin, pressed my face to the welts. I kissed him all over, licked along the lines I'd raised and then made him roll back over, so that I could bob my mouth along the length of his cock.

Oh, fuck me, he was so hard and raw and sweet, and I let my mouth love him until I could hold back no longer. I stared for one moment at his cock, wet and slick from my mouth. Then slid my panties aside and climbed astride him, a dangerous version of the image I'd had in the bar, with him cradling me, holding me up. Now I was on top of him, pushing him down.

I slipped up to the head of his cock and then rode my way back down. I pushed up on my thighs, feeling the ache in the muscles, and then slammed myself against him. Our eyes met. Our gaze held. I let him know with a look when I was ready for him to come. I knew he would never release before I gave him permission.

His body shuddered with the power of his climax, and I took myself to the edge on his pleasure. Coming a beat after him, coming with the belt still by my side on the bed, those silver studs muted in the lamplight from the table.

"You were right," I told him, looking at the man on my mattress. The man with his arms bound over his head. His body limp and used and relaxed. A grin spread over my face. I knew what he was seeing when he looked at me. "How's that?" he asked, as I moved to set him free. I felt comfortable releasing him. I knew he'd be coming back for more.

I kissed the spot above his leather cuffs, and then rubbed the skin with my fingers.

"It's all in the wrist."

MISTRESS OF CARABAS

D. L. King

I own Carabas. It's the kind of place that's both comfortable and decadent. I find my regulars like it that way—dark and chic and plush and a little on the Goth side—because I like Goth. People either like it or they find somewhere else to be. But regulars at Carabas never complain because, really, where else would they go?

I schemed and bribed and filled out miles of paperwork to get my cabaret license, which is, in and of itself, an amazing feat. But it's what I do with that cabaret license that's really amazing. A cabaret license, in New York, means dancing is allowed, among other things. No cabaret license; no dancing. It's something only a New Yorker would understand.

In point of fact, customers don't actually dance at Carabas; it's more about watching other people "dance."

"Cute," you say. Yeah, yeah, well, whatever, but getting back to my story...

How did Libby Cox become the Mistress of Carabas? I suppose it was all due to my boy, Kit.

We both wound up at a mutual friend's dinner party and it was lust at first sight. Kit was gorgeous in his silk shirt and leather pants and black Spanish ankle boots, still is, actually, but this isn't really a story about Kit; it's a story about my becoming what I was always meant to be and making everyone, including Kit, happy in the process.

We made our excuses to the dinner party host around ten and caught a cab over to my place. Once in the door, I immediately set to unbuttoning his shirt. I think I said something like, "Get those boots and pants off," and he replied, "Yes, Ma'am," and took them off. Just like that. Then he stood there, hands clasped behind his back, shirt half-unbuttoned and otherwise naked from the waist down.

After a brief pause, I stepped back and gave him a thoughtful look. More slowly I said, "Finish taking off the shirt now."

My sweet, beautiful, submissive Kit did exactly as he was told and resumed his easy stance while his eyes practically burned a hole in my brain. Still clothed, I slowly circled around him, coming back to the front, and picked up his thickening cock. There was an almost electric charge at my touch; I thought I smelled ozone and what had been taking its time became stiff almost at once.

I'd had my share of boys, but I'd never experienced this kind of sublime submission. It was as though a chorus of angels began singing as I slowly bent the beautiful Kit over a chair and flogged him red, before taking him in the ass. From that time on, we were practically inseparable. Kit went everywhere with me unless I told him to stay behind or had him running errands. But I think from the first, he wanted to make me over, and believe me, I was ripe for a makeover.

The night of our one-year anniversary, I had Kit bound tightly to the bed and had just begun to torture him when he said, "You should do this." I must have stopped and looked at him peculiarly because he said, "No, this is what you should do."

"Well, perhaps you hadn't noticed, my pretty Kitty, but I am doing this," I said as I placed another clip on his straining cock.

"No, no, I mean you should do this for real, like for a living."

"That's awfully sweet, but I think it's a little too late to think about becoming a pro domme now."

"I'm not making myself understood. Sometimes it's difficult when I'm hard."

"Yes, baby, I know. So little blood to the brain and all," I said.

He grinned, and then winced when I added another clip. "I'll explain later, just remind me if I'm too far gone, because this is important." And he settled back into the play.

Once his hips began to writhe against the bed, I used my tiny graphite cane to smack his skin. His "oooohs" and "aaaahs" joined the motion of his hips, and I could tell he'd forgotten all about whatever it was he'd wanted to say earlier.

That's the way things should be. When I play with a boy, I want him focused only on the moment and his body—and mine. If he's thinking about the ball game score or what he wants for dinner, what's the point? A good sadistic scene is a work of art for all to enjoy.

Kit loves my brand of pain, almost as much as he loves my pussy, and once I'd settled that over his eager mouth, we were both exactly where we wanted to be. His well-trained tongue and teeth hit all the right spots, but after my first orgasm, I began thinking about what he'd said earlier, so as he worked feverishly to bring me to a second climax, I pinched his nipples hard, letting him know he could come, too.

After indelicately climbing off his face and removing all the clips to the sounds of his little shrieks and whimpers, I untied him and cuddled him close. Soon he began to purr for me.

"All right now, what was all that stuff about 'doing something' about?"

"Well," he said, "you're so beautiful and confident, you know, and I get hard just thinking about you."

I kissed his sweaty temple.

"I think a lot of people would feel the same."

"I told you I wasn't going to become a pro domme," I said. I got up and began to dress. "Put some pants on and let's have some cake."

"Why do I have to put pants on?"

"Because I said so."

Kit got out of bed and did as he was told.

I love to watch that lean, muscular ass of his moving around in jeans. Some guys look great naked, and I'm not saying Kit doesn't, because he does. I especially love his naked ass when it's red and puffy with my strap-on entering it. But I think he looks his hottest when he's shirtless, barefoot and wearing jeans. I don't know why that is. Maybe those tight, stonewashed blue jeans draw attention to his bottom so nicely that I feel the need to rip them off.

"I wasn't talking about being a pro domme," he said. "But I know you like doing this more than real estate. You should have a place of your own. Lib, you should open a club."

I followed him into the kitchen and sat at the table while he served the cake and champagne. "Of course, I like sex more than real estate. Who wouldn't? And that's an interesting idea, but I don't know shit about running a club."

"I'll run it for you. All you have to do is be there and do what you do. The market's crap right now. You said it yourself. Look, what do people spend their money on when they don't have any? Movies and bars. Entertainment. This is the perfect idea."

Even though I thought he was nuts, the idea stayed with me for weeks. I'd be showing an apartment for the twentieth time, thinking how fast I used to be able to turn them over, and Kit's idea would pop into my mind and I'd wonder if this social worker, looking at the apartment, would get his rocks off in a club like that. What about that lawyer last week? Yeah, definitely the lawyer...

Kit has a way of making things happen. He's attached himself to me, and I'm not complaining. But if he thinks I need something or should have something, he just goes off and makes it happen. He likes to ensure my life is comfortable because he knows if it is, his will be too.

As I was finishing up not renting the apartment for the twenty-first time, I got a text from Kit, asking me to meet him at some Brooklyn address. "Brooklyn!" I shot back. "Just come," his reply read.

The address was in Williamsburg; not a bad train ride from Manhattan and a very hot location. (I sound like a real estate agent even to myself.) It was in an industrial, rather than residential area, and the loft spaces were large.

"It's perfect," he said. We were on the top floor of an eight-story loft building. "Big, affordable, zoned for commercial use and we have exclusive access to the roof! Check out all these columns!" He raced over to one of the columns supporting the high ceiling and stood with his back to it, legs spread, arms over his head, as if cuffed to a bolt in the column, and flashed a Cheshire cat grin.

With a wicked smile, I slowly walked over to him and grabbed his crotch. "Where's the agent?" I whispered. His eyes became slightly unfocused.

"She's here," he said. "You're the agent."

"No, I'm not." My hand squeezed him a little tighter.

"Yes, you are," he said, in a slightly higher pitch. "Your agency represents the building and I asked for you."

That's my Kit; not only does he find the perfect property, but I get the commission, too!

Six months later, Carabas opened. In less than a month, we had a line at the door every weekend. Unbelievably, we were in the black within five months.

Carabas is not a bar. It's not even just a cabaret; it's very much more than that. In front, you'll find fine dining. The style is ultra-modern molded concrete, steel and black glass. Cylindrical steel light fixtures hang from the ceiling at various heights and candles adorn the tables, providing a twilight ambience. The walls are sparsely decorated with modern erotic watercolors. The wait staff is all male. They wear tuxedos and Harlequin half-masks.

Further in, you'll find a lounge area with cushy leather sofas and chairs, low cocktail tables and a sound system providing a Gothic throb. The lounge is warm, with subdued lighting and a color scheme of browns and reds. Boys and girls, in tight-fitting outfits with high necklines, long sleeves and bared bottoms, wait tables. Columns are ubiquitous throughout the space, so we've put them to use in the lounge. There, each column is spotlighted with a boy or girl fastened to it.

While none of the moving sculptures are completely naked, they are all in various forms of undress and are tied or shackled in revealing postures. All clothing and accessories are white as it makes for a nice contrast with the padded brown leather upholstery covering the columns.

The roof affords an amazing view of the city. Patrons can

relax in our outdoor cigar lounge where they can take advantage of one of our bootblacks or bring their own, if they like.

The restaurant stops serving at eleven, which is when things begin to heat up. Beyond the lounge area is the real reason for our success, and what Kit had in mind when he began to put all the wheels in motion. The back room contains an intimate theatre with cozy love seats and club chairs surrounding a raised stage, where all the "dancing" is done.

Attendance at the grand opening of Carabas was by invitation only and Kit was the featured performer. After dinner, followed by an open bar in the lounge, our guests took their seats in the darkened theatre. When the spotlight hit the stage, there I stood, with Kit kneeling at my feet. I wore a butter-soft black leather skirt and a blue silk corset. I've always liked the way those two colors go together, and they have such great connotations. Kit wore a black leather jock strap and matching leather collar and cuffs. The jock framed his bare ass nicely but of course, it was just a bit of costuming for the warm-up.

The stage was built around one of the many columns in the loft, and this column had the eyebolts imbedded in it that Kit had playfully imagined when he first brought me to the space. I led him to the post and clipped his wrists to a bolt above his head, then fastened his ankle cuffs to bolts in the floor, spreading his legs a bit. The black waistband and leg bands of the jock made his white ass practically shine under the spotlight.

Using a short whip, I began to systematically cover his bottom, the backs of his thighs and his upper back with small red marks that soon turned to raised welts. When I began, I could sense the audience and hear some low voices. I could hear their breathing and the little noises they made in response to the action on stage, but by the time I began to raise welts on

Kit's back it was all about the two of us. Everything else disappeared, leaving Kit and me in our own little island of light and all I could hear was the crack of the whip, Kit's breathing and my own heartbeat.

After a while, I knew I was finished with his back. Carrying the whip, I walked the five feet between us and gently caressed the welts on his bottom. His sigh at the touch of my fingers prompted me to slide my hands up his sides and around his chest while I licked the welts on his back, tasting the salt from his sweat. I could feel him melt at the touch of my tongue and sense the complaint when I moved away from him. I unfastened his ankles and turned him around, facing out, before refastening them.

Although he looked at me with love and desire, I could tell he was entering that unfocused, floating state. I could relate. I felt much the same way, or at least I imagined it was much the same way. Kit's pain is my pleasure, but I had to be in control. It's a fine line between creating deep and abiding pain for him and assuring that he isn't hurt. I have to stay focused. I can't allow my own pleasure to carry me too far from Kit's pain.

I took a moment to cover his eyes with a heavy black leather blindfold. It assured he wouldn't be distracted by the audience, but also served to protect his eyes. I kissed his mouth and stepped back. He strained his head forward to follow me but I was already gone.

Once back where I'd been, I drew back my arm and let the whip fly again, this time making contact with his thigh. He jumped and gasped. He continued to make little noises as I covered the fronts of his thighs in more small red welts. When I was satisfied, I moved up to his chest and covered the area around his navel and watched his muscles contract each time a strike would fall. Then I moved up to his chest, covering the entire area, with the exception of his nipples, which had been raised to sharp, little points. He'd been moaning and making little mewing noises for quite some time and I couldn't help but make a few yummy noises of my own. My last two strokes were reserved for those stiff buds of flesh and as I let the whip fly to bite into each nipple, in turn, the sound of his scream made my juices gush until my panties were soaked.

I put the whip down and went to lick his poor, punished flesh. His breath came in rasps as, standing to the side, I removed his jockstrap. His cock had been erect for some time, but now that it was no longer imprisoned, it strained forward, red with a deep purple head. His balls were tight and I could tell he was on the edge. I knew it wouldn't take much to push him over, but keeping him in this state was a powerful aphrodisiac for me. I ran an index finger up the underside of his cock to the tip. His hips danced and tried their hardest to jerk away from me. Then, as I stroked him to orgasm, I had enough presence of mind to allow the audience a good view. I heard gasps and then a few giggles when a fountain spurted forth. As I removed his blindfold, I heard the applause.

After unfastening the clips on Kit's ankle cuffs, and then his wrist cuffs, I hugged him to me. Both of us were flying and, though I knew we were on a stage, in front of an audience, that scene was one of the most intimate of my life. Once I felt certain Kit could stand on his own, I let him go and turned toward the applause. People were actually on their feet, still clapping. I looked at Kit and he grinned back at me.

Carabas would be a success.

There are two shows a night on the weekends. We have a variety of tops and bottoms who perform, but my beautiful Kit dances on that stage at least once a week, under my hand. At other times, if I see a boy in the audience who particularly catches my eye, I may call him up to dance for me as well. Most often, however, I can be found strolling through the club, with Kit on a leash at my side, greeting regulars and making small talk.

THE UNIFORM
AND THE ROPE

Fulani

The important thing," Robert says, "is that you feel a Zen calmness. This isn't just being tied up for sex—it's an art form in its own right."

Right.

My interest in things Japanese has brought me to this suburban house, sparsely furnished, tidy and tasteful apart from garish *hentai* posters on the walls. They're Japanese, yes, but they suggest complex, deviant interests rather than Zen calmness. *Hentai* is a shortened form of the term *hentai seiyoku*, meaning "sexual perversion."

Having learned to create ikebana, wear a kimono convincingly, and appreciate the subtleties of calligraphy (though not write it, which takes years of practice), I've come to experience the seamy underside of Japanese erotic sensuality. This is something everyone knows about—because the DVDs and magazines are everywhere—but few people can do properly because, like ikebana or calligraphy, it takes years of practice.

Shibari. Japanese bondage.

I'm wearing my best, difficult-to-obtain Japanese schoolgirl uniform. Japan doesn't share Western tastes for leather, rubber and PVC. Everything is cutesy, "schoolgirl" doesn't have the same connotations as it does in this country, and the kinkiest sex toy you can have is a bagful of rope…

Hence, over my school uniform and causing some disturbance to it, I'm wearing *karada* and *shinju*. *Karada*: the classic diamond-pattern body harness. *Shinju*: binding above and below my breasts, compressing them slightly. At the same time my forearms are drawn behind my back, fingers of the left hand touching my right elbow and vice versa.

"There's no need to bind the wrists," Robert explains. "You can't move your arms to defend yourself or reach the knots anyway."

I like the way the rope holds me, the embrace and constraint of it. I'm entranced by the pressure across my breasts, between my legs, and elsewhere too. It hits sensitive spots, erogenous points I didn't know I had, all over my body.

"Where did you learn to do ropework?"

I'm imagining a trip to Japan, months apprenticed to a *nawashi*—a bondage teacher.

"Oh," he says airily, "reading books, going to bondage workshops, and I went to Shibaricon a couple of years back."

I try not to let my disappointment show. I was hoping for some kind of…what? Authenticity? Robert doesn't appear concerned by his un-Japanese learning. He hums to himself as he adjusts the ropes.

"In Japan," he says, "there are maybe half a dozen guys recognized as Rope Masters, though it's a very subcultural thing. Midori once said even the liberal arty crowd thinks of bondage as something that's only practiced by sexually immature people."

I know who Midori is, because he's lent me copies of her books.

So I'm tied up, secure or helpless depending on point of view, beginning to get a rush from the tightness of the ropes. And that means I'm sexually immature?

Doesn't feel that way to me.

"There are two or three Rope Masters in this country, too, but I wouldn't remotely qualify as one. Even if I *am* kind of well known in bondage circles..."

He's attached a rope from the back of the *shinju* to a hook in the ceiling, and while he's been talking he's lifted me three or four inches, just enough that my toes can reach the floor but not my heels.

"There's a history to Japanese bondage," my not-Rope Master tells me. "They didn't have manacles and chains. The police used rope to secure prisoners. Each area had its own traditions and methods. But the culture made it a no-no to tie higher status people with knots, so they used loops instead. Now, with bondage, it's the same. You only ever use a couple of simple knots. There's just the one in the entire *karada* you're wearing. And the *shinju* ends in the length of rope that's holding you on your toes, though for safety I have tied that one off..."

He's being geeky, but meanwhile he's winding another rope around my left leg. When he stands up, he threads the tail end through another hook and pulls. This means my leg is held up as though I'm in mid-prance.

"Asymmetrical, you see. Symmetry is too easy, you never see it in Japanese art. It's the same with ikebana." This is true; the classic flower arrangements are rarely symmetrical.

I feel a gentle push. Only my right toes are in contact with the floor, and I spin slowly. The semi-suspension makes the ropes tighter now around my breasts. I draw concentration inward, trying to deal with the sensations, adjust to them. My breathing is shallower, more focused. I'm more conscious of my own heartbeat, the blood in my veins. At first it's a constellation of tiny, teasing caresses. Then, the way a constellation suddenly has a shape and a name, some of those pressures feel stronger than others, more insistent, a not-quite-painful pleasure like a thumb pushing into aching muscles. Unforgiving cords probe and press unrelentingly between my legs. It feels weird and hot at the same time.

He carries on talking as though this is normal conversation. Maybe it is for him.

"Of course, up until the 1800s, bondage was often used as a form of torture for criminal suspects. There was a method that twisted your legs into a lotus position and then pulled your body down onto your legs. The 'Prawn', they called it. It interferes with circulation and cramps the muscles. Then there was a face-down suspension with weights on your back, which would have pulled all the joints in your body."

"You're telling me this because...?"

"Just because," he says smugly. He knows he's putting images of pain in my mind, a not-so-subliminal message that ropework isn't just about tying the victim down for fucking. And these mental pictures are mingling with the strange pleasures my body is telling me about. I wriggle experimentally.

If I arch my back and push my hips forwards it sends shivers from my pussy all the way to the top of my head...

"The term *shibari* is recent, from the verb 'to tie'. Originally it was called *kinbaku*, which translates as 'tight binding' with a subtext of 'erotic ropework.'"

I don't care what it used to be called. I'm getting hot and bothered, breathing fast, wondering vaguely if the fact my eyes won't focus is due to raw excitement or lack of oxygen. My eyelids close of their own volition. In the darkness, the rope holding my body becomes a latticework of pleasure. I can feel the juices, the moisture, gathering in my panties.

"It's an open question how much history and tradition there is in *shibari*. It didn't become a big deal in Japan until the 1950s or 1960s. Even then, it was a secretive, underground thing. By the seventies it appeared in some sex clubs, but that was done for show. You'd have a performance—princess meets bandit who throws a few ropes on her, pulls her clothes off, waves a sword around, fucks her. Fun, but no real technique. It's only in the last twenty or so years it's become popular, and actually a lot of the people who've developed 'Japanese' bondage have been based over here."

This is a mindfuck. He's got me to this point and only then told me it's not what I thought it was. It's not an ancient secret art; it's a modern invention that isn't even really Japanese.

His hand is warm on my ass. My skirt is bunched around my waist due to the ropes that are also chewing at my pussy. "You know," he chuckles, "you're not so traditional either. A real Japanese schoolgirl should have white panties, not a black thong..."

Mixed-up images in my head. Pain and princesses and bandits, flogging and spanking and fucking. I try to concentrate, but I'm dizzy with desires the ropework is creating in me.

"Princess. Bandit. Spank! Fuck?"

That's good enough. It conveys my needs.

He spins me again. I lose all sense of where I am.

"Think of it this way. The Japanese part comes in the aesthetics. You, in bondage, become an artwork. There's a balance and tension between the immobility of your body and the discovery that even quite small movements will eventually give you an orgasm."

Eventually?

My belly grinds hard against the rope, my pussy tries to close around it, my clit is huge and compressed and almost in flames. My thighs flex and pump as though gripping an invisible lover.

I have no more words. Just a throaty, needy growl.

"Schoolgirl princess wants to be spanked and fucked?" I open my eyes to see him looking down at me, as though I've asked for something not quite proper. Like he's a bondage expert and I'm a kinky little brat.

He is and I am.

Hands caress my aching breasts. With the ropes in place there's no way to pull off the blouse and bra. Instead, he pinches my right nipple firmly, through the material.

The sharpness of the pain makes me take shorter, harder breaths.

Tiny movements of fingers, pushing and pulling on my nipple, draw my whole body into a swaying motion that yet again squeezes and burns against pussy and breasts.

I'm drawn into the movement, the ache and promise and promiscuity of it.

"You know," the Rope Master murmurs in my ear, "that uniform you're wearing: the origins of it are English. It was introduced in the 1920s, when a private women's college adopted the style of Royal Navy uniforms. One does wonder why that might have happened—college teachers having a penchant for smartly turned-out sailors...But for a real school, your skirt is *way* too short. It's a delinquent girl gang skirt..."

The sudden slap of male hand on bare female backside sends sharp and complicated shocks up and down my body that interact with the sensuous pain of the ropes.

He's not gentle. My ass reddens quickly and I'm bouncing and twisting in the ropes, pulled by one nipple, bucking with each slap, while he pours liquid lewdness in my ear.

"You can think you're a princess, but to me you're a smutty little deviant, a rope slut, pain toy and fuck-doll in a school uniform you're seven or eight years too old to wear...Those who wear the uniform that way are often delinquents. And delinquents...they need to be punished, don't they?"

Tears start to roll down my cheeks. I can't tell if they're the result of pain, pleasure or the mix of emotions caused by the mindfuck.

It doesn't matter.

The spanking goes on for...I don't know, my sense of time is screwed. When he's done, Robert sweeps my foot from under me so I swing in midair, shaking, feeling the ropes biting against skin. Every shiver in my body is magnified by the bondage. He knows this. He's enjoying it.

He ignores my pain and pleasure. He makes green tea. Sips from a thimble-sized cup. Watches me in my art, my performance, my climax.

When the convulsions die down, he releases me from the rope keeping my body upright. I crumple into his arms, am carried to the cool firmness of the futon. He doesn't remove the other ropes. He uses a penknife to dispose of my thong, pressing the cold blade against my flesh in symbolic threat-promise-anticipation. He moves the ropes so they run around rather than between my pussy lips. He pulls the labia apart, gratified at how juiced I am. And he fucks me, firm and unhurried at first, gathering pace and strength.

"Next time," he murmurs, "We'll try an upside down suspension, and a flogging."

Next time? Yes. Please. But right now I only feel abandonment and restraint and exhilaration. I absorb his thrusts, his fierce domination, my submission to the ropes and...and...

I come hard, long, a shuddering fit that leaves me comatose. Later, when the aftershocks have subsided, we lie together and watch some old tentacle porn, but that's another story.

ABOUT THE AUTHORS

MORGAN AINE has been penning poetry, short stories, and erotica for many years. Her erotic writing has been showcased at various websites such as *ERWA, AmoretOnline, Adult Story Corner,* and *Emerald Collection.* She lives beside a large lake in the Southern United States.

ANNA BLACK's erotic fiction has been published in *The MILF Anthology* and *Cowboy Lover—Erotic Tales of the Wild West.* Her stories have also appeared in two of Zane's erotic anthologies: *Purple Panties* and *Honey Flava.* She writes for Ellora's Cave under the name Jenna Reynolds.

RACHEL KRAMER BUSSEL (rachelkramerbussel.com) is an author, editor, and blogger. Her books include *Spanked; Naughty Spanking Stories 1* and *2; Yes, Sir; Yes, Ma'am; He's on Top; She's on Top; Caught Looking; Hide and Seek; Crossdressing; Rubber Sex; Bedding Down;* and the nonfiction collections *Best Sex Writing 2008* and *2009.*

STEPHEN ELLIOTT is a former stripper and the author of six books including *Happy Baby*, a finalist for the New York Public Library's Young Lion Award. His most recent book is an almost all true sexual memoir called *My Girlfriend Comes to the City and Beats Me Up*.

Erotic short fiction by **A. D. R. FORTE** appears in the anthologies *Lips Like Sugar*, *Lust*, *Best Women's Erotica 2008*, and *Yes, Ma'am*. Forte's stories have also been featured in several *Black Lace: Wicked Words* collections.

FULANI started writing erotica in 2008. His first full-length BDSM novel, *The Secret Circus of Pain and Degradation* was published by Pink Flamingo in 2010 and a collection of original stories appeared in 2011 under the Renaissance Sizzler imprint. He blogs at fulanismut.blogspot.com.

SHANNA GERMAIN's (shannagermain.com) work has appeared in *Best American Erotica*, *Best Bondage Erotica 2*, *B Is for Bondage*, *Best Gay Romance 2008*, *F Is for Fetish*, *J Is for Jealousy*, *Got a Minute?*, *Hide and Seek*, *Naughty or Nice*, *Caught Looking*, and *Slave to Love*.

TERESA JOSEPH is a bisexual writer from England whose perverted perceptions and wicked sense of humor earned her third place in the Rauxa Prize for Erotic Writing 2006.

MIKE KIMERA was raised as an Irish Catholic in England and now works as a management consultant in Switzerland. His work has been included in multiple anthologies. He was a winner of the Rauxa Prize for Erotic Writing. His short story collection *Writing Naked* was published in 2005.

D. L. KING publishes the review site, Erotica Revealed. Editor of *Where the Girls Are, The Sweetest Kiss, Spank* and *Carnal Machines*, her stories can be found in *Please, Ma'am, Sweet Love, Fast Girls* and *Yes, Sir*, among others. Find her at dlkingerotica.com.

JAMES WALTON LANGOLF is a part-time college student living out in the sometimes still wild west. You can find additional work in *Love at First Sting, Surreal* magazine, and *Apex Science Fiction and Horror Digest*. Contact her at Jameswlangolf@gmail.com.

JAY LAWRENCE is an expatriate Scot who currently hangs out near Vancouver, Canada. She is the author of over a dozen erotic novels and many short stories that have appeared in publications on both sides of the Atlantic.

JESSICA LENNOX has lived coast to coast, and currently resides in New Jersey. Her hobbies, interests, and obsessions include gender theory, motorcycles, travel, sports, and, of course, books. Jessica's erotic fiction has appeared in *Best Women's Erotica 2008* and *Tales of Travelrotica for Lesbians: Erotic Travel Adventures, Volume 2*.

NIKKI MAGENNIS (nikkimagennis.blogspot.com) You can find her work in various anthologies including *Yes, Sir; Love at First Sting; E Is for Exotic; J Is for Jealousy; Sex in Public;* and *Sex with Strangers* Her second erotic novel, *The New Rakes*, was published in November 2008.

SOMMER MARSDEN's (SommerMarsden.blogspot.com) work has appeared in numerous anthologies. Some of her favorites include *I Is for Indecent*; *J Is for Jealousy*; *L Is for Leather*; *Spank Me, Tie Me Up, Whip Me*; *Ultimate Lesbian Erotica '08*; *Love at First Sting*; and *Yes, Sir*. Sommer lives in Maryland.

N. T. MORLEY is the author of more than fifteen novels of erotic dominance and submission, including *The Office*, *The Nightclub*, and *The Castle*, as well as many published erotic short stories.

TERESA NOELLE ROBERTS' erotic fiction has appeared in *Naughty or Nice?*, *B Is for Bondage*, *F Is for Fetish*, *H Is for Hardcore*, *Caught Looking*, *Hide and Seek*, *Best Women's Erotica 2004, 2005*, and *2007*. She also writes erotica and erotic romance as half of the writing team known as Sophie Mouette.

CRAIG J. SORENSEN's erotica has been published online in *Clean Sheets*, *Oysters & Chocolate*, *Lucrezia Magazine*, and *Ruthie's Club*. He lives in rural Pennsylvania with his talented family.

DIANA ST. JOHN lives in a small town nestled in the foothills of the Sierra Nevada Mountains in Northern California with her husband and children. Diana blogs regularly about sex and spirit at skinprayers.blogspot.com.

RAKELLE VALENCIA, has co-edited four erotic anthologies, of which *Rode Hard, Put Away Wet* was a finalist for a LAMBDA Literary Award. She has had many erotic short stories published, which can be found on the bookshelves of the most excellent bookstores. She was also a 2006 semi-finalist in the *Project: Queer Lit Contest*.

XAN WEST is the pseudonym of a New York-based BDSM and sex educator and writer. Xan's work can be found in *Best SM Erotica 2*, *Got a Minute?*, *Love at First Sting*, *Best Women's Erotica 2008*, and the forthcoming *Men on the Edge*, *Leatherman*, *Backdraft*, and *Daddies*.

ALLISON WONDERLAND (aisforallison.blogspot.com) has a B.A. in Women's Studies, a weakness for lollipops, and a fondness for rubber ducks. Allison's erotica has been published at ForTheGirls.com and is anthologized in *Wetter, Island Girls*, and *The Longest Kiss*.

ABOUT
THE EDITOR

Called a "literary siren" by Good Vibrations, **ALISON TYLER** is naughty and she knows it. She is the author of more than twenty-five explicit novels, including *Tiffany Twisted*, *With or Without You*, and *Melt With You*, and the winner of "best kinky sex scene" as awarded by *Scarlet* magazine. Her novels and short stories have been translated into Japanese, Dutch, German, Italian, Norwegian, Greek, and Spanish.

According to the website Clean Sheets, "Alison Tyler has introduced readers to some of the hottest contemporary erotica around." And she's done so through the editing of more than fifty sexy anthologies, most recently *With This Ring, I Thee Bed* (Harlequin).

Ms. Tyler is loyal to coffee (black), lipstick (red), and tequila (straight). She has tattoos but no piercings; a wicked tongue but a quick smile; and bittersweet memories but no regrets.

In all things important, Ms. Tyler remains faithful to her partner of more than fifteen years, but she still can't settle on one perfume. Visit alisontyler.com for more luscious revelations.